P9-CFL-531

THE STAR

Junior Novelization

Adapted by Tracey West

Simon Spotlight

New York   London   Toronto   Sydney   New Delhi

If you purchased this book without a cover, you should be aware that this book is stolen property. It was reported as "unsold and destroyed" to the publisher, and neither the author nor the publisher has received any payment for this "stripped book."

This book is a work of fiction. Any references to historical events, real people, or real places are used fictitiously. Other names, characters, places, and events are products of the author's imagination, and any resemblance to actual events or places or persons, living or dead, is entirely coincidental.

Sony Pictures Animation

SIMON SPOTLIGHT
An imprint of Simon & Schuster Children's Publishing Division
1230 Avenue of the Americas, New York, New York 10020
This Simon Spotlight paperback edition October 2017
TM & © 2017 Sony Pictures Animation Inc. All Rights Reserved.
All rights reserved, including the right of reproduction in whole or in part in any form.
SIMON SPOTLIGHT and colophon are registered trademarks of Simon & Schuster, Inc. For information about special discounts for bulk purchases, please contact Simon & Schuster Special Sales at 1-866-506-1949 or business@simonandschuster.com.
Manufactured in the United States of America 0917 OFF
10 9 8 7 6 5 4 3 2 1
ISBN 978-1-5344-1753-3 (hardcover)
ISBN 978-1-5344-1461-7 (pbk)
ISBN 978-1-5344-1462-4 (eBook)

Chapter One
An Angel Appears

A long time ago—nine months B.C.—a tiny rodent scurried through the dusty streets of Nazareth. The rodent's name was Abby, and she was very hungry.

There was nothing much to eat in the desert. But Abby knew the city was filled with humans, and where there were humans, she could find food. She hopped on the back of a traveling cart and stayed out of sight during the bumpy ride through the city gates.

When the cart reached a busy street, Abby hopped off. She scampered to the top of a stone building and sniffed the air. The smell of freshly baked bread reached her nose.

Abby jumped off the building and landed on the back

of a woman on the road. The woman let out a scream and swatted at Abby with her broom. The little rodent quickly ran off, following the smell.

She stopped in front of a small house. She'd found it! She climbed through the window and spotted a young woman pulling a loaf of bread out of the stone oven.

The woman had long, brown hair and kind, dark eyes. She put the bread on the table and folded her hands in front of her. She closed her eyes and whispered a soft prayer of thanks for the food.

Abby saw her chance. She quickly grabbed the loaf of bread and began to drag it away. Then, suddenly, she found she couldn't move.

She looked behind her and saw the woman looking down at her. The woman's finger was planted in the bread. Abby froze.

"Don't think I don't see you, little one," the woman said.

Abby bolted and hid behind a pot. She shivered as the woman walked near her, towering above her.

But the woman didn't hurt Abby. She tore off a chunk

of bread and put it on the floor next to Abby.

"I think there's enough for both of us," she said with a kind smile.

Suspicious, Abby slowly approached the bread. The woman closed her eyes and returned to her prayer. Abby grabbed the bread and quickly stuffed a piece into her mouth.

She was enjoying her meal when the sound of rumbling thunder distracted her. A rush of wind blew through the room, and a shadow fell across everything.

Then a voice spoke. It was a voice that didn't sound like any human Abby had ever heard.

"Mary."

The woman, Mary, looked at Abby. "Was that you?" she asked, but the little rodent shook her head.

Hundreds of candlelike flames appeared in the room, descending from the ceiling. Mary stood up, wide-eyed.

Abby stared at the lights too. She didn't know *how* she knew, but she knew what she was looking at—an angel.

"Fear not," the angel told Mary, "for you have been favored by God to receive and bear a son."

Abby dropped the bread she was eating and stared at the angel, stunned.

"A son?" Mary asked. "But . . . how?"

"The Holy Spirit will overshadow you and the child will be called the Son of God," the angel replied. "For nothing is impossible with God."

"Thank you," Mary said. "Do I say thank you? Yes. I mean, yes."

The lights began to swirl together, forming a wave. The wave of light wrapped around Mary, and then shot out the window with the speed of a comet.

Abby and Mary both ran to the window. A brand new star glittered brightly in the sky.

Tears of joy filled Mary's eyes. Abby looked down at the morsel of bread in her paw. She tossed it away. Then she hopped outside.

"Guys! Guys!" she cried, running through the streets of Nazareth. "You're not gonna believe this!"

Chapter Two
The Donkey's Plan

All over the land, people noticed the new Star shining brightly in the sky.

So did the animals.

In the middle of the desert, three camels were resting for the night when the Star appeared.

"Whoa!" the camels said.

Out in the pastures, a flock of sheep looked up from grazing when the Star began to shine.

"Whoa!" they cried.

In the city of Bethlehem, a goat, a cow, and a horse saw the Star from their stable.

"Whoa!" they exclaimed.

Some desert mice popped out of their holes in the sand.

"Whoa!" they squeaked.

"Whoa!" said a cat next to them. Frightened, they scampered back into their holes.

Back in the city of Nazareth, a small donkey and an old donkey were hitched to a grinding wheel in a mill. The donkeys walked around and around in circles all day long. As they walked, they turned a big wheel that ground wheat into flour.

Even though it was nighttime, the donkeys were still walking in circles. The owner of the mill was so mean that he rarely let them rest. He hadn't even given them names. He just called them Little Donkey and Old Donkey.

Every time they walked around the circle, the donkeys would get a quick glimpse of the outside world through a small knothole in the wall. Little Donkey was passing by the knothole when he saw the brand new Star shining through it.

"Whoa!" he said, stopping. "Okay, you're not going

to believe this, but I think a new star just appeared in the sk–"

Before he could finish, the wheel turned, pulling Little Donkey away from the knothole. Old Donkey was pushing behind him, trying to get him to move.

"No, no, no," Old Donkey said. "What have I said about looking through that thing?"

Little Donkey tried to back up. "Oh, come on, wait! This doesn't happen every day!"

Old Donkey pushed back. "Well, you know what does happen every day? Work! Remember that? That thing we do every day? Walking in circles around the mill for the rest of our lives until we die?"

"You have a beautiful way with words, you know that?" Little Donkey asked.

Instead of backing up he ran forward. The wheel spun quickly, and Old Donkey had to move fast to keep up with it. Soon Little Donkey was back in front of the knothole again.

"There's nothing out there for you, kid," Old Donkey said, panting.

But Little Donkey had a good feeling. "Things are changing," he said. "That Star means something. And I'm not gonna be here forever."

The two donkeys walked in circles until the Miller let them stop. In the morning, they were back at work again. Little Donkey was still thinking about the Star when a dove swooped into the mill.

"I love the smell of freshly ground grain in the morning!" the bird said.

Old Donkey rolled his eyes. "Hey kid, your unemployed bird friend is here."

Little Donkey perked up. "Dave!" He ran around the mill, yanking Old Donkey behind him, and stopped underneath the dove.

"Hey, pal!" Dave greeted him.

"What's new out there today?" Little Donkey asked.

Dave hopped down onto the grinding wheel and began gobbling up the grain. "Oh, not a whole lot. I mean, it's Nazareth. You know, that rooster on Fifth Street overslept again. And that horse, uh, what's his name? Jeremiah or Hezekiah or something–he lost a shoe. And then, well, it's barely worth mentioning, but the, uh . . . the Royal Caravan is strolling through town today."

Little Donkey's mouth dropped open in surprise. "What? The Royal Caravan? Are you kidding?!?"

Dave hopped up onto Little Donkey's snout. "No, buddy, for real!" he said happily. "I spotted them outside of town and had to come straight here to tell you!"

"Today's the day we've been waiting for!" Little Donkey cheered.

"Nazareth can kiss my gleaming white tail feathers good-bye!" Dave added. He shook his butt in Little Donkey's face.

Little Donkey blew Dave off his snout. "See, I told you that Star was a sign!" he said. "We're meant for something greater than this."

Old Donkey snorted. "This is our job. And once you accept that, you'll be a glowing picture of happiness, like me," he said. But he didn't look or sound happy at all.

"Uh, we're talking about the Royal Caravan here," Dave said.

"It's the ultimate job!" Little Donkey said with a

dreamy look in his eyes. "You get to go from town to town. See the world. Visit important people. And you get to march with the biggest, strongest, greatest horses in the world!"

Dave flew back onto Little Donkey's head. "All the animals in every town, watching us go by, and chant-ing our names."

"We'll finally be doing something important," Little Donkey added.

Old Donkey shook his head. "Hmph! A miniature donkey in the Royal Caravan. That'll be the day."

"Don't listen to him," Dave told Little Donkey.

"And what's a dove gonna do, carry one grape at a time?" Old Donkey asked.

"Hey, at least he's not locked up in a mill like us!" Little Donkey pointed out.

Dave looked at Little Donkey. "I'm telling you, folks in this town just don't get it!" he said. Then he turned to Old Donkey. "And I can carry two grapes, one in each talon, thank you very much."

A rumbling sound came from the distance. Dave flew

up to the rafters, looked outside, and smiled.

"Bells! That's them!" he cried. "It's time to activate Operation Prison Break!"

Little Donkey and Dave had worked out the plan already. In order to escape, Little Donkey needed to cut the ropes that connected him to the wheel. There was a sharp metal thing on a stick in the corner of the mill. (It was called an ax, but Little Donkey didn't know that.) The ax could cut the rope, if Little Donkey could get it in the right position.

Little Donkey began by dragging a bucket near his path. Then the moving wheel pulled him away from the bucket. He ran to catch up with it again.

Then he slowed down. He grabbed the ax with his teeth, and leaned it on the bucket.

"Okay," he said. All I have to do is kick this sharp, metal killer stick toward my head and duck!"

"It'll cut your harness!" Dave said.

"And I'll finally be free!" Little Donkey added.

Dave grinned. "Oh, I love Operation Prison Break. Such a good idea!"

Little Donkey took a deep breath. "Here we go!"

He confidently kicked the bucket supporting the ax. The sharp tool flipped up, but not toward Little Donkey. It flipped away from him, knocking over a bucket on a shelf, and landed on a table.

The shelf came crashing down, and the bucket rocketed across the room. It smashed into a rack of bread, which fell onto a ladder.

"That's not good," Little Donkey said.

The ladder knocked over a spade, and the sharp digging tool chopped the rope in half that was holding up a hanging lantern. The lantern swung and smashed an oil lamp, shattering it and spilling oil onto a wood shelf. The shelf burst into flames!

Little Donkey blew on the fire, trying to put out the flames. It didn't work. The flaming shelf toppled over, knocking into a table. A knife, ax, and pitchfork on the table launched through the air!

The knife and pitchfork whizzed by Little Donkey's ears. The ax got even closer–and sliced right through his rope! He was free!

"See? I knew that would work," Little Donkey said proudly.

"Just like we planned!" Dave said. "With a momentary death hiccup."

Dave flew past Old Donkey, waving. "Well, old timer, it's been real. Good luck to you."

Little Donkey followed him to the door, but stopped. He looked at Old Donkey.

"Wait, Dave. We can't just leave him," Little Donkey said.

"Oh, come on!" Dave cried. "Buddy, I get where you're coming from, but this is the Royal Caravan, not the *Retirement* Caravan. Look at him—he's, like, three hundred years old!"

At that moment the mill door swung open, knocking Dave aside. The Miller, a stocky man with a mean face and bushy eyebrows, eyed the damage in the barn. He grabbed a bucket of water and quickly put out the fire. Then he removed a yoke from the wall. He slipped the heavy wood collar around Little Donkey's neck and attached it to the wheel.

Through the open door, Little Donkey saw the Royal Caravan moving away. His one chance at freedom. His one chance to do something important. He sighed.

The Miller slapped him on his hindquarters, so Little Donkey would get moving again. He took a few slow, sad steps forward.

Then he felt angry. He turned to the Miller. "You're nothing but a great big, rotten, good-for-nothing bully!" he yelled.

But all the Miller heard, of course, was the braying sound of an angry donkey.

"Hee-haw! Hee-haw! Hee-haw!"

The Miller rolled his eyes and left, closing the door behind him.

"Yeah, you better walk away!" Donkey yelled after him.

Dave fluttered down from the rafters.

"Aw, who needs the Royal Caravan," Dave said. "There's plenty of excitement here in Nazareth."

Dave held back tears. "I'm gonna be honest—I'm very upset right now. I'm gonna go find someone to poop on."

Dave flew away.

Little Donkey still felt angry. "If that Miller thinks this yoke is gonna stop me, ooh, boy, do I have a surprise for him! I'll be riding with kings any day now, you'll see!"

But getting rid of the heavy yoke was a lot harder than cutting the rope that had been holding him before. A month went by. Then another. And another.

Six months later, poor Donkey was still pushing the wheel and longing for a better life.

Chapter Three
Donkey Breaks Loose

Before the angel Gabriel visited Mary, she had pledged herself to marry a man named Joseph. Now, six months later, her wedding day had arrived.

Joseph stood in front of his home, wearing a flower crown on his head and waiting for Mary. He hadn't seen her for months, and he'd missed her. She had gone to Judah to help her relatives Elizabeth and Zechariah take care of their new baby, John. Joseph felt nervous about the big day, and was talking to himself.

"Mmmm, still no Mary," he muttered. "Okay. Just a little late. It's normal to be late to your wedding feast. Totally normal. Just like it's normal to talk to yourself."

Then he saw Elizabeth and Zechariah approaching, riding in a wagon drawn by donkeys. Elizabeth held Baby John in her arms. Mary wore a white wedding shawl over her blue dress.

Joseph smiled as Mary jumped out of the wagon.

"Mary, you look beautiful!" he said, taking her hands.

He placed a crown of flowers on her head that matched his own.

"So do you," Mary replied. "Well, handsome. I've missed you."

"You're a little late, you know," Joseph said. "I was starting to worry."

"Sorry, our fault, we're always late," Zechariah apologized.

Elizabeth approached, holding the baby. "'We' who?" she teased. "You were driving!"

She looked at Joseph. "Mary was such a big help to us these past months," she said. Then she smiled at the baby. "Wasn't she, Baby John?"

Joseph kissed the baby on the head. "Sorry, big guy," he said. "I know how great she is, but I'm taking her back."

He took Mary's hand and led her to the gate of the courtyard behind the house.

"Joseph, there's something I want to talk to you about," Mary began.

"Of course," Joseph said.

She stopped and looked into his eyes. "Just warning you, it might be a lot to take in."

"Mary, of course, it's our wedding feast," John said kindly. "You can tell me anything."

Mary was about to speak when the gate swung open, and a woman saw her.

"She's here!" the woman announced.

The gate opened wider, revealing all the friends and family who had gathered for the wedding. They all stood up and applauded the wedding couple.

"Sorry, what did you want to talk about?" Joseph asked.

"Oh, it can wait," Mary said. "Let's enjoy the party."

While Mary and Joseph began their wedding celebration, Little Donkey plodded around the mill wheel. He sighed.

"So, uh, any new escape plans, kid?" Old Donkey asked.

"What's the point?" Little Donkey replied. "I already missed my chance to join the Royal Caravan. And I'm still stuck on this same old wheel, with the same old view."

That view, of course, was Old Donkey's tail.

"What's wrong with the view?" Old Donkey asked.

Little Donkey just sighed again. He stopped in front of the hole in the wall and peered through it.

"I know it feels like we're just going in circles," Old Donkey said.

Little Donkey stared at Old Donkey. "We are."

"Look, kid, we're mill donkeys," Old Donkey said. "We grind grain. We don't carry kings."

Little Donkey nodded. "Yeah, I should have listened to you and given up a long time ago."

His whole body sagged, and he slowly made his way around the wheel again. Old Donkey looked at the smaller donkey, and the harness connecting the two of them. As he passed by the knothole, he looked through it and saw the outside gates were open.

Old Donkey hated seeing his little friend so sad. But maybe, just maybe . . .

"Aaaaaaaah!" Old Donkey cried, dropping his head and kneeling on his two front legs.

The wooden harness around Little Donkey's neck tipped forward. He slipped right out of it.

"What's happening?" Little Donkey asked, trotting up to Old Donkey.

"Kid, it's my leg," Old Donkey said, grimacing in pain. "Go get help!"

Little Donkey went to the door and started braying loudly. *"Hee-haw! Hee-haw!"*

The Miller burst in.

"These good-for-nothing animals," he muttered. "What is it now?"

Then he spotted Old Donkey on the floor and frowned. "Oh good. Just what I needed," he complained.

Old Donkey stopped yelping and looked at Little Donkey. "Are the gates open?" he asked.

Little Donkey looked over at the gate. It was wide open!

The Miller turned to Little Donkey. "You! What are you doing out of your harness?"

Old Donkey suddenly jumped up and lurched forward. The wheel of the mill swung around.

Wham! It knocked the Miller to the ground. Little Donkey gasped.

"Kid, get outta here!" Old Donkey yelled.

"What about you?" Little Donkey asked.

"I'll be fine," Old Donkey assured him. "I just hope you find what you're looking for."

That's when it hit Little Donkey. Old Donkey had faked falling down! He wanted Little Donkey to escape.

"I don't know what to say," Little Donkey said.

"You're welcome, kid," Old Donkey replied. "Now get going!"

Little Donkey ran as fast as he could toward the open gate. The Miller stood up.

"Oh no, you don't!" he yelled, his face turning red with anger.

But before he could take a step, Old Donkey swung the mill wheel around again.

Wham! It sent the Miller flying backward.

"You're free, kid!" Old Donkey yelled. "Make it count!"

Little Donkey shot Old Donkey a quick, grateful look and then raced away as fast as he could.

Chapter Four
The Chase Is On!

Dave the dove was perched in a tree, trying to charm a female dove.

"Look, I'm not gonna be here long," he was saying. "I have bigger plans, but–"

He stopped at the sound of a loud voice yelling below him.

"Runaway donkey! Somebody grab him!"

Dave looked down. It was the Miller! He was chasing Dave's good friend, Little Donkey! He had escaped!

Dave took off, quickly catching up to Little Donkey. He flew over his friend's head.

"You broke out! Yes, the dream is back on. Woo-hoo!" he cheered.

"Not free yet!" Little Donkey said, gasping for breath. "The Miller's on my tail!"

Dave looked behind Little Donkey. "Yeah, and he does not look happy."

"I am *not* happy!" the Miller barked.

"Follow me!" Dave told Little Donkey. "Let's get out of town!"

Dave looked around for a way to get away from the Miller. Up ahead, workers were repairing a house. A wooden ramp led to the roof.

"This way, up here!" Dave cried, zooming toward it.

"No, no, not up!" Little Donkey yelled. "Donkey don't like up!"

He looked behind him. The Miller was gaining on him. He had no choice.

He ran up the ramp. It collapsed under his weight as soon as he got to the roof.

The frightened workers fixing the roof screamed and darted out of the way as Little Donkey charged past them.

"Sorry, sorry," Little Donkey said. "I'm really a nice guy."

On the street below, the Miller raced around the house, keeping his eye on Little Donkey. The donkey had just surprised a worker holding a bucket of paint.

"Get out of the way!" Little Donkey yelled desperately. He couldn't slow down. But the worker was frozen in fear.

Little Donkey ducked and scooted under the man's legs. The worker teetered, and tumbled off the roof. He landed on the Miller, and the paint splashed over both of them.

Then Little Donkey reached the edge of the roof. He skidded to a stop.

"What now?" he asked Dave.

"Jump!" Dave yelled.

"Jump? What? Are you crazy?" Little Donkey replied.

Dave looked down. The Miller was now climbing up the ramp.

"JUST JUMP!" Dave yelled.

Little Donkey made a face. He leaped off the roof . . . and crashed through the roof of the chicken coop below!

"Aaaaaaah! A flying donkey!" one of the chickens squawked.

Then the Miller, covered in paint, crashed through the hole in the roof too. Little Donkey and Dave raced out of the coop as the chickens jumped and cackled, sending loose feathers floating into the air.

The donkey and the dove raced through the house, past a family eating their midday meal. The Miller came after them, followed by the angry chickens.

Little Donkey and Dave burst out into the street and made their way through the crowds. They turned a corner—and found the Miller standing there, waiting for them!

"Other way! Other way!" Little Donkey yelled.

He scrambled backward, tumbling down a flight of stairs that led to a crowded square.

"Dave! Dave! Where are you?" he cried.

He backed up again, smashing into a cart and knocking it over. The canvas top fell onto his body. He shook it off, but a rope attached to the canvas was wrapped tightly around his leg.

Little Donkey couldn't get away. He climbed on top of the fallen cart and searched the square. The Miller was speeding toward him.

"Oh no, no, no!" Little Donkey wailed.

"There's no way out of this," the Miller growled.

Little Donkey was in a tough situation. He looked down from the top of the cart. If he jumped to the other side, he might be able to get away. But the rope was still attached to his leg.

He thought about going back to the mill, about pushing that wheel day in and day out . . .

. . . and he jumped.

The rope yanked at his leg and snapped loudly. The rope broke, and Little Donkey fell to the ground.

He stood up, wincing in pain. Something was wrong with his leg, but he had to keep moving. He spotted an open gate, and hobbled toward it.

Little Donkey had escaped the Miller . . . for now.

Chapter Five
A Name for Little Donkey

After the wedding feast, Mary approached Elizabeth. Mary looked down at her belly, which held the baby that had been growing inside her ever since she was visited by the angel. Elizabeth knew about the baby— but Joseph didn't.

Mary took a deep breath and nodded toward Joseph. "Okay. Here goes."

"He's a good man," Elizabeth said. "He'll understand."

"Thanks," Mary said, and gave Elizabeth a hug.

"Zechariah!" Elizabeth called to her husband. "Party's over!"

Zechariah froze, a muffin halfway to his mouth. He

stuffed it into his pocket and went to join his wife.

"Great party, guys!" he called out. "Joseph, you must be the happiest man in the world!"

Elizabeth frowned at him.

"Second happiest!" Zechariah corrected. "Clearly I'm the happiest."

Mary and Joseph smiled and waved as Elizabeth and Zechariah left the courtyard.

"Well, this place isn't gonna clean itself," Joseph said. "I'm starting with the dishes!"

Joseph loaded his arms with dishes and walked up the steps to the house.

"I'll start down here!" Mary called up to him. Then she looked down at her belly. "Where I'll figure out how to tell him about you."

She took another deep breath. "It's all good news, I promise," she practiced saying. "All good news."

A rattling noise behind her made her jump. She turned around, but didn't see anything.

She heard the noise again. This time when she turned, she saw a pitcher shaking on top of one of the tables. She crouched down to lift up the tablecloth—and found herself face-to-face with a donkey!

"Oh!" Mary gasped.

"*Aaaaaaaah!*" Little Donkey brayed.

He darted out from under the table, pulling off the tablecloth and sending everything clattering to the ground.

"I'm caught again!" he said, panicking. "There's gotta be a better hiding place."

He tried to run, but Mary noticed that one of his legs was badly hurt. He limped behind a basket, trying to hide from Mary. But he was much bigger than the basket.

"Okay, maybe not here," Little Donkey said.

He limped behind a clay pot even smaller than the basket.

"Not that one, either," he said. As he moved away, he knocked over the pot, breaking it.

The only other object he could hide behind was a goblet that had fallen to the ground. He limped behind it and scrunched up his body as small as he possibly could.

Why couldn't I be smaller? he wondered. *The one time I wish I were smaller!*

Mary slowly removed the goblet. She noticed the rope still tangled around Little Donkey's back leg.

"You poor thing," she said. She gently reached for the rope and unraveled it from his leg. Little Donkey winced when she touched him, and Mary realized that his leg must be broken.

"You're hurt!" Mary said.

She got up and ran to Joseph's carpentry workshop, and returned with two small pieces of wood.

"That can't be good," Little Donkey said.

Mary tore a strip of cloth from her shawl. Little Donkey didn't like the sound. He cringed and started squirming.

"If I am going to help you, you're going to have to let me, okay?" Mary asked gently.

Little Donkey calmed down. Mary used the cloth to wrap the two pieces of wood around his broken leg.

"Better?" Mary asked.

He stood up. His leg still hurt, but not as much as before. He grunted in agreement.

Mary ran a hand through his mane. "Nice to meet you. I'm Mary."

Just then, Joseph came back down the stairs.

"You didn't tell me you had a donkey," Mary said.

"I don't," Joseph said. He came toward Little Donkey, who stumbled backward, frightened.

"He must be a stray," Joseph said. "Go on, boy. Shoo!"

He clapped his hands. Then he got behind Little Donkey and tried to push him toward the gate. But Little Donkey didn't budge.

"Scrappy little donkey," Joseph muttered. "All right. That's how it's gonna be."

He rolled his shoulders, cracked his knuckles, and tried to push Little Donkey again.

Little Donkey quickly stepped to the left, dodging him. Joseph fell face-first into the dirt.

As Joseph picked himself up, he heard Mary behind him.

"Are you okay?"

"Yep, I'm fine," he replied. "Just a little–"

He stopped. Mary hadn't been talking to him. She

was talking to the donkey! Little Donkey was looking at Mary with wide, innocent eyes.

"The poor little guy is hurt," Mary said. "Give him a break."

Joseph cupped his hands around his mouth. "Hello? Did somebody lose a donkey? Because if you have, he's here!"

Mary smiled at Little Donkey and petted his mane.

"What should we call you?" she asked. "How about . . . Boaz?"

Joseph turned back to Mary. "Wait, what are you doing? You're naming it?"

"What do you think, Bo?" Mary asked Little Donkey.

Little Donkey nodded, thinking. "Bo," he said out loud, but of course Mary couldn't understand him. "No one has ever given me a name before."

He smiled at Mary.

"I like it!"

Chapter Six
A New Home for Bo

Joseph, Mary, and Bo all walked to Joseph's carpentry workshop. Joseph shook his head. "No, Mary, if you name him, you're going to start feeling affectionate toward him. And once you feel affectionate, you're going to want to keep him. And if there is one thing we are definitely NOT going to do, it's—"

He turned to see that Mary had already made a little home for Bo inside his carpentry workshop. Bo was snuggled in a basket with blankets. Mary had placed her flower crown on his head.

"That's my workshop!" Joseph protested.

"Let's just let him stay here until he's all better," Mary said.

She removed her shawl and covered Bo with it. For the first time, Joseph noticed her pregnant belly.

"Mary?" he asked.

Mary turned and saw the look in his eyes. "Come on, let's go talk upstairs."

Bo watched Mary and Joseph walk away. He liked the nice lady who had helped his leg–but he wasn't about to be cooped up again. He wanted to be free!

"Okay, I'm outta here," he said.

Still weak and hurt, he hobbled across the courtyard. He tried to push the gate open with his head, but it wouldn't open. He tried pushing it with his butt next–and it still wouldn't open.

Then Dave landed on top of the gate.

"There you are!" he cried happily. "I'm so glad you're okay. Do you know how much flying around I've done looking for you? I thought that maybe the Miller caught you and was gonna eat you."

"Eat me?" Bo asked. "Yeah, I don't think he was going to do that."

"You don't know!" Dave countered. "He had crazy in

his eyes. So keep it down! He's still out there someplace!"

Suddenly Bo felt worried. "That guy was yelling about a donkey. Do you think he heard?"

"No, I think we're good," Dave assured him. "This is the last place he'd check. Nothing special ever happens in an old shack like this."

In the house, Joseph was taking in the news Mary had given with him.

"The Messiah?" he asked. He pointed to Mary's belly. "You're saying that baby is actually the Messiah? Like, from the prophets? I need to sit down."

"I know, I know how it sounds, but yes!" Mary replied. "And God wants you and me to raise him."

"Me?" Joseph asked. "Are you sure I'm . . . I mean, did the angel mention me?"

Mary answered truthfully. "Well, no, but–"

"I can't raise the Son of God!" Joseph cried, panicked. "He's a king! I'm just a carpenter. He needs someone with a little more experience being . . . I don't know, king-ish? I mean, who am I?"

Mary took his hand in hers. "You're my husband."

They looked into each other's eyes.

"I'm sorry," Joseph said. "This is just so much to take in right now. Can I have a little time?"

Downstairs, Bo and Dave were trying to open the gate. Bo took a few steps back so he could get a running start. But his bad leg gave out before his head could hit the door.

"Hate to say it," Dave said, "but even if we got you out, you're never gonna make it to the Royal Caravan on that leg."

Bo thought about that. "Dave, I don't want to hold you back," he told his friend. "You fly ahead without me. I'll catch up once my leg heals."

Dave flapped his wings. "No, we're in this together!" he insisted. "I'm not gonna leave you here. Friends don't do that."

"Are you sure?" Bo asked.

"Yeah, and besides, you'd never make it without me," Dave said. "I am a bird of the world. I know how things work out there. You are a donkey of the barn. A very small, ill-smelling barn. You need me."

Bo nodded. "Okay. So now what?"

"Hide out there until your leg heals," Dave replied, "and then just get yourself kicked out and we'll be back on track, pal!"

"Bo, actually," Bo told him. "My name is Bo now. Mary named me."

"Bo. That's got a nice ring to it," Dave said. Then he suddenly became suspicious. "Wait—that lady-person *named* you? I said *hide* here. Not settle in and get a name. Have I taught you nothing?"

"I am not settling in," Bo assured him. "Once my leg is healed, it's time for Operation Kick Me Out."

"Good. Now, I'm an expert at this kind of thing, so listen up," Dave said. "Things I've found that tend to tick people off: jumping out and scaring them, singing really loudly early in the morning, staring at them while they eat, and telling them their baby is funny-looking."

Bo and Dave talked until night fell, and Bo settled into the workshop. Dave fell asleep, perched on the fence.

In the house, Joseph anxiously paced back and forth,

worried, while Mary slept. Then something caught his eye through the window–the brightly burning Star. That Star had appeared six months ago, when Mary said the angel visited her.

A brand new star, Joseph thought. *That's a miracle.*

He looked down at Mary, sleeping peacefully on the bed. He sat down and grasped her hand. Her eyes fluttered open and he smiled at her.

He was ready for another miracle.

Chapter Seven
Three Wise Men . . . and Their Camels

Three months later, three camels moved through the desert. Morning had dawned, but the bright new Star could still be seen in the sky overhead.

Riding on the camels were three special passengers–wise men from a land far away.

The camels talked as they walked.

"You guys ever remember walking this far?" complained Felix, a camel with short brown fur.

They shook their heads.

"I thought we were going to make a left two deserts ago," complained Cyrus, a strong camel with shaggy white fur.

"I can't believe we passed that last oasis," added

Deborah, a camel with big brown eyes. "I'm getting thirsty."

Felix gazed up at the rider on his back. "Maybe they're lost."

"Wise men don't get lost," Deborah argued.

"True," Felix said. "So they must know where this birthday party is."

"What makes you so sure it's a birthday party?" Cyrus asked.

"Uh, have you seen the gifts these guys are bringing?" Felix replied. "Gold. Myrrh. Frankincense."

"Could be a baby shower," Cyrus said. "You bring gifts to a baby shower."

Felix shook his head. "Not frankincense. What's a baby gonna do with frankincense? It's gotta be a birthday party!"

"What if it's not a party at all?" Deborah piped up. "What if we're on our way to do something important. Like . . . meet the Son of God?"

"You do need a drink of water," Felix told her. He looked at Cyrus. "She all right?"

"Gotta get her out of this sun," Cyrus said.

The camels kept walking until they reached the city of Jerusalem. They arrived at the palace of King Herod, where guards led them into the royal courtyard.

King Herod sat on his throne. He had a gray beard, and wore red robes of the finest silk, decorated with gold. He was reading an official scroll and frowning.

"I don't know why the emperor needs to count all his subjects," the King complained. "But if a census Caesar decrees, then a census he will get."

He turned to the army commander at his side.

"Send the Royal Guard to round up every man and woman," he said. "Let the counting of the sheep begin."

The commander bowed and hurried away, as the King's chamberlain–the manager of the palace–approached him.

"Your Majesty, three magi are here bearing gifts for the King," he reported.

The wise men got off their camels and walked up to King Herod, holding their gifts. The camels huddled together in the back of the courtyard. They were eyeing two scary-looking dogs chained up nearby. The dogs barked and growled at the camels.

"Hold it right there, camels!" barked Thaddeus, a sleek, sharp-looking dog.

"C'mon, Thaddeus, do the thing," panted Rufus, a big, muscled bulldog. "Give it to 'em!"

"All in the timing, Rufus," Thaddeus said.

He paused. Then he started barking fiercely!

"Rrowf! Rrowf! Rrowf!"

The frightened camels jumped back.

"Ooh, I got chills," Rufus said.

"Your turn," Thaddeus said.

Rufus glared at the camels. "Watch out, 'cause I'm a mangy mutt and I'm crazy!"

He began to bark, but he sounded like a teeny dog, not a big, scary one.

"Yip! Yip! Yip!"

The camels blinked at him, confused.

Rufus grinned confidently. "Nailed it!"

Thaddeus shook his head. "Just do what I do."

"RROWF! RROWF! RROWF!"

The camels scurried behind a pillar.

"Yeah, chew on that!" Rufus taunted them. "Next time you want something . . . chewy."

A hunter yanked the dogs away. Up at the throne, King Herod studied the gifts the wise men had brought.

"Your gifts are unexpected, though not unwelcome," the King said.

The three wise men looked at one another.

Balthazar, a skinny man in purple and gold robes, spoke up first. "Um, Your Majesty, these gifts are not for you."

"They're for the new King," added Melchior, who had a long, curly brown beard.

King Herod's eyes narrowed. "What new king?"

"The one foretold by the Star," replied Caspar, the third, and oldest, wise man.

The camels listened in as the wise men told the story of the appearance of the Star, and that they believed it meant the birth of a new King.

"I knew it! It's a birthday party for the new King!" Felix said triumphantly.

"No, no, I'm pretty certain it's a baby shower," Cyrus said.

"Or maybe they're talking about the coming Messiah, the Son of God," Deborah chimed in.

Cyrus looked at Felix. "I'm starting to worry about her," he said.

Felix turned to Deborah. "Are you okay? How many hooves am I holding up?"

Deborah rolled her eyes and looked back at the King. He called over to his chamberlain and whispered to him.

"What are they saying?" Felix asked.

"I can't make it out," Cyrus said. "Something about–"

"Yo!" Felix interrupted him. "Look at that guy! You see him?"

The Hunter walked in front of them, holding the two dogs by their chains.

"Oh, he's just the royal dog walker," Cyrus said. "Trust me, Felix. I know these things."

"What? Dog walker?" Felix asked. "He's like a nightmare wearing a helmet!"

Deborah nodded. "And look at that knife!"

Felix's eyes narrowed. "He's a killer."

Then King Herod clapped his hands.

"We must find this King at once," he said. "I will set my scribes to the task."

He smiled at the wise men. "In the meantime, I invite you to stay in the palace as my royal guests."

The wise men looked at one another, unsure about the King.

"No, that's not necessary, sire," Balthazar said.

Now the camels looked at one another.

"Okay, that was sinister," Cyrus said.

"Yup, we're leaving," Felix agreed.

But before they could escape, the guards surrounded them.

"Too late," Deborah said.

The guards led the camels and wise men away. King Herod waved his hunter over.

"This new King is a problem," he whispered in the Hunter's ear. "Get rid of the problem."

Rufus and Thaddeus began to bark excitedly.

The hunt was about to begin!

Chapter Eight
The Hunt Begins

After seeing the angel Gabriel appear to Mary, Abby the rodent had begun traveling from town to town, spreading the word about what she had seen. On a desert highway outside Jerusalem, she spoke to a group of rodents gathered under a cart.

"The room was filled with magical light!" Abby told them. "And then the angel said that the child would be the new King!"

The rodents gasped. "Wow!"

"And I thought, 'I'm not ready to be a mom!'" Abby said. "But then I realized that the angel was talking to the lady."

Suddenly, the rodents she was talking to scattered. Abby frowned.

"Wait, wait, I'm not done!" she cried. Then she sighed. "That's usually everyone's favorite part."

Whomp! The next thing she knew, a big paw clamped down on her tail, pinning her to the ground. Rufus the bulldog grabbed Abby and dangled her in front of his face.

"Nice story, rat!" he growled. "Here's how it ends."

He popped Abby into his mouth!

"THE END!" he said, with his mouth filled with the poor creature.

"Rufus, spit it out!" Thaddeus scolded. "We need that rat to talk."

Abby popped out of Rufus's mouth. "I am *not* a rat. I'm a pygmy jerboa," she told them.

"What's a jerboa?" Rufus asked.

"It's still in the rodent family but an entirely different species," Abby answered.

Rufus sucked Abby back into his mouth.

"Rufus, enough!" Thaddeus yelled. "Spit it out."

"Aw, I was just starting to get a little bit of the flavor," Rufus complained.

Thaddeus growled at him, and Rufus knew he'd better obey. He spat out Abby, but before she could run, Thaddeus clamped a paw on her.

"You've been telling your story to every critter in Galilee," he said. "Now it's our turn to hear it. From the beginning."

"From the beginning?" Abby squeaked. She gulped and started her story. "Okay. So, I was born in a sack of barley somewhere in Capernaum . . ."

"Skip to the end!" Rufus barked. "Who's the woman?"

"Her name is Mary," the terrified rodent replied. "She lives in Nazareth. But please don't hurt her. She's really nice!"

"Don't worry. We're harmless," Thaddeus said, with a wicked grin. Then he lunged toward Abby.

"Hey, that's mine!" Rufus yelled, pushing Thaddeus aside. "I already got my germs all over it!"

Thaddeus growled and pushed Rufus. While the two dogs scuffled, Abby started to run away. But the Hunter appeared. He grabbed her by the tail and dangled her in front of his face.

Then he tossed her over his shoulder. Relieved, the pygmy jerboa ran away.

Oh no . . . Mary! she thought. *I hope those mean dogs don't find her!*

Chapter Nine
Operation Kick Me Out!

Bo had lived with Mary and Joseph for three months. He had to admit, it was a lot better than being at the mill. Mary fed him and took care of him. And it was fun watching her belly grow. The baby was almost ready to be born.

One morning, Mary took the wood boards off Bo's leg and wrapped it in just the cloth.

"Looks like you're healed up!" she said. "Feeling better?"

They were outside, in a donkey pen Joseph had built for Bo that was connected to his carpenter's workshop. Joseph was busy packing bundles of clothing and supplies into a large cart.

"All I'm saying is it's unfair," Joseph complained to

Mary. "You know, to make all these people drop every-thing for the census. And for us to travel to Bethlehem, especially in your condition."

"Joseph, I'm not dying," Mary said. "It's just a little road trip. We'll be fine."

She sat on a stool and leaned back against the fence. Bo walked up to her and she rubbed his belly. He closed his eyes and smiled.

"You know, most donkeys have to work," Joseph said. "You're spoiling him."

He leaned over and whispered in Bo's ear. "She's spoiling you!" Then he headed upstairs to get another bundle.

Dave flew into the workshop and landed near Bo.

"Hey, look at you!" he cried. "Your leg's all better."

"Hey, Dave!" Bo greeted him.

Dave perched near Bo's ear and whispered to him. "All right, time to activate Operation Kick Me Out!" he said. "What's your plan of attack?"

"Uh, first I thought I'd let her finish this belly rub," Bo said lazily.

"Snap out of it!" Dave cried. "A little bird named Methuselah told me the Royal Caravan will be passing through not too far from here! We can catch them if we leave soon."

Bo hopped to his feet. "All right. Let's get kicked outta here!"

Joseph dropped the last of the bundles into the cart. "All packed up! Is the donkey ready?" he asked.

Bo and Dave looked at each other, both thinking the same thing.

Ready for what?

Mary stood up. "Yep! His leg looks good as new."

"Finally!" Joseph said. "Time for him to earn his keep."

He picked up a rope lasso and faced Bo. Bo crouched and glared at him.

"All right, Bo," Joseph said calmly. "Let's get you hitched up to this cart so you can take us to Bethlehem."

"Bethlehem!" Dave cried. "Not good, not good. The Royal Caravan is nowhere near Bethlehem!"

"Don't worry," Bo said. "He's got to catch me first."

Joseph tried to throw the rope around Bo's neck, and Bo darted out of the way. Joseph tried again, but Bo just moved out of the way again.

Mary tried to help. "Joseph, maybe if you just–"

"Don't worry, Mary. I've got this," Joseph said firmly.

Bo backed farther into the pen.

"Well, looks like you got me," Joseph said. He turned and acted like he was giving up. But then he whirled around and lassoed Bo around the neck!

Joseph gave a triumphant cry. "Come here! Ha!"

Bo looked down at his neck and realized that he'd been caught. He glared at Joseph and quickly moved back, pulling Joseph right into a fence post. *Bonk!* Joseph banged his head.

"Ooh, that looked like it hurt!" Mary said.

"It did," Joseph replied, rubbing the top of his head.

Bo looked at Dave. "How was that?"

"Look out!" Dave yelled.

Joseph ran to Bo and grabbed him by the rope around his neck. He dragged Bo over to Mary.

"See? Under control," Joseph said.

Bo pulled back again, and Joseph fell to his knees.

"Joseph!" Mary cried in alarm.

Joseph stood up. "No, no. I'm okay."

"You know, we can walk to Bethlehem," Mary said. "No problem."

Joseph scowled at Bo. "Useless donkey."

He slipped off the rope around Bo's neck and walked over to the cart, followed by Mary.

"Nicely done!" Dave congratulated Bo.

"I thought so," Bo said. "Did you see how I laid him out on the ground?"

"Those caravan horses have nothing on you!" Dave told him.

"Okay, so now what?" Bo asked.

"Easy," Dave replied. "All we have to do is slip through the gate when they're on their way out."

They looked toward the gate–and saw that Mary was already closing it.

"No, no, no! Don't close the gate!" Bo yelled.

He ran toward the gate, and Mary closed it in his face with a chuckle.

"I know, I'll miss you too," she said. "Don't worry. We'll be back soon."

Bo banged on the gate with his head, but it was too sturdy to break through. As he watched Mary and Joseph disappear in the distance, a wave of sadness came over him. But it wasn't because he had missed his chance to join the Royal Caravan.

It was because he was going to miss Mary. He'd been so distracted by Dave's escape plan that he'd forgotten how nice Mary had been to him. How she took such good care of him, and healed his leg, and rubbed his belly.

"I guess that was good-bye," Bo said with a sigh.

"You're not gonna cry, are you?" Dave asked, flying up to the gate. "Come on, we've got to figure out a way to open this thing!"

Chapter Ten
The Dance of the Royal Dove

Bo and Dave didn't have much of a plan. Bo kept head-butting the gate, and Dave kept trying to lift the latch with his beak. Neither method was working.

"This is what I get for having a friend who can't fly," Dave muttered. "You know what, gates were never a problem before I met you!"

Bo looked around the pen and at Joseph's carpentry workshop. "There's something we can use here," Bo said. "There's that table, that lumber, those tools . . ."

Dave was staring bug-eyed at the courtyard gate. "And that giant knife!" he yelled.

A shiny, curved knife was sliding through the crack

between the door of the gate and the frame. Somebody was breaking in!

"Hide!" Bo yelled.

He scrambled behind some crates near Joseph's workshop. Dave landed just above him. They watched as a big man with two scary-looking dogs entered the courtyard.

It was the Hunter, Rufus, and Thaddeus. The dogs had led their master to Nazareth, and he had asked around to find out if there was a woman about to give birth to a child. Eventually, he'd found his way to Mary and Joseph's house.

The two dogs sniffed the air.

"Okay, Bo, what haven't you told me?" Dave whispered. "You been making some new friends?"

"No," Bo replied. "I bet the Miller sent them to bring me back to the mill."

Then Dave noticed something. "They left the gate open behind them!"

"I'll make a run for it!" Bo hissed. "Dave, you jump out and create a distraction. You're good at that."

"What? No, terrible plan," Dave said. "Why don't *you* make the distraction and *I* run for it?"

"Because I'm the only one trapped in here, and you can fly anywhere you want!" Bo reminded him.

Dave nodded. "Good points."

Bo started to creep along the fence, hoping the dogs wouldn't notice him. They sniffed across the courtyard.

"I got a scent!" Rufus announced. "I smell . . . a dog! Thaddeus, there's definitely a dog around here!" Then he sniffed his own paw. "Oh. I smell me."

He grinned at Thaddeus, who glared at him.

Dave flew to a fence post near them.

"Hey, scary dogs, you guys here for the show?" he asked.

The dogs spun around and saw Dave.

"What show?" Thaddeus asked.

Dave laughed. "What show, the silly dog asks. You're adorable," he quipped. "The Dance of the Royal Dove, of course! Played in Rome. Six years. Great reviews. Caesar saw it twice. Made him cry, but he won't admit that because, you know, he's Caesar and all that, but he definitely cried. Like a baby."

Thaddeus growled impatiently. "We don't have time for this."

"No, no, no, wait! The show is about to start!" Dave pleaded.

The dogs ignored him and started heading in Bo's direction. Dave took a deep breath and started to sing.

"Ba, ba, dop, bee, bop a, boo, bop!"

Then he started to dance, flapping his wings and bobbing his head.

Bo stopped in his tracks and stared at Dave.

"What are you doing?" Dave hissed at him. "Don't watch me!"

Dave's plan was working. Both dogs stopped to stare at the sight of the strange bird making weird noises and doing a crazy dance.

Bo crept toward the gate. Thaddeus's head spun around and he spotted him! Both dogs charged Bo, cornering him.

"Where's your owner?" Thaddeus asked.

"What he said!" Rufus added.

"Who, the Miller?" Bo asked. "I–I don't know any Miller. Never met the guy. My owner's a nice pregnant lady. You would love her!"

"*That's* who we want!" Rufus cried.

"Where is she?" Thaddeus asked.

Bo was surprised. "Wait, you're looking for Mary?" he asked. If these scary dogs were looking for Mary, he didn't want them to find her. "Did I say pregnant lady? No, my owner's a miller. Really. I'm just a mill donkey on vacation. Who's Mary?"

"Keep talking," Thaddeus demanded.

Dave flew over and landed on Bo's shoulder. "Okay, that was pathetic. Let me handle this, Bo."

He faced the dogs. "Guys, donkeys are stubborn. He's not gonna tell you anything!"

Bo nodded. "Yep. Sorry, guys."

"You would have to torture it out of him," Dave said.

Bo's eyebrows shot up. "Wait, what?"

The Hunter came out of the shadows and stomped toward Bo. He grabbed him by the mane. He leaned his face close to Bo's.

Then the Hunter noticed the cloth bandage on Bo's leg. The dogs sniffed it.

"He didn't bandage himself," Thaddeus said.

"That's her scent!" Rufus exclaimed. "Now we just gotta figure out which way she went!"

The Hunter let go of Bo. Rufus and Thaddeus ran toward the gate, then stopped and looked at Bo.

"We'll tell her you said hello," Thaddeus said threateningly.

Then the two dogs barked at the Hunter and ran off. They were on Mary's trail.

Bo watched them, horrified. *What are they going to do to Mary?*

Dave landed on Bo's back. He didn't realize that his friend was worried about Mary.

"Woo! They left the gate open!" he cheered, doing a happy dance.

A pigeon called down to Dave from a nearby railing.

"Hey, Dave! Way to shake your tail feathers, bro!"

Dave looked at Bo. "Let's get out of here."

Chapter Eleven
Which Way?

Dave rode on Bo's back as the donkey trotted through the streets of Nazareth. They reached a fork in the road.

Dave pointed left with his wing. "Okay, the Royal Caravan is this way. We'll catch it in no time."

Bo paused. Then he headed right instead of left.

"Wait, where are you going?" Dave asked. "Dream is that way." He pointed left again.

"Right," Bo said, "but Mary is *this* way."

Dave shook his head. "Oh no, no. The Royal Caravan cannot wait for a rescue mission. Especially when that guy is after her. He is major bad news."

"I'm not just gonna let her get hurt, Dave," Bo said. "She was nice to me."

"Oh, I see. She was nice to you," Dave said. "Nice? I'm nice! I humiliated myself back there so we could break out and join the Royal Caravan!"

Bo walked past a fence post. A group of pigeons laughed at Dave and pointed.

"Hey, Dave! Heard you've got some impressive dance moves!" one of them called out. The other pigeons snickered.

Dave flew over to them. "Yeah, yeah, real funny, Jeff," he replied. "You're bitter because pigeons are just ugly doves!"

Then he flew back to Bo. "Come on, Bo, we've been waiting for this," he pleaded.

"It'll just take a second," Bo promised. "Once Mary's safe, we'll turn right around and join the Royal Caravan. Deal?"

Dave hesitated. "Fine. Deal. So we turn *right* around," he said. "Leave this to me. I know a shortcut."

Bo and Dave headed to the city gate. Bo squeezed

under it, and they walked toward the road to Bethlehem.

They didn't know it, but they were being watched. The Hunter's dogs had lost Mary's trail at the gate. But Thaddeus knew that Bo would try to find Mary. So they waited until they spotted Bo to see where he would go.

"He'll lead us right to her," Thaddeus said.

"And then what?" Rufus asked.

"Then we find the baby," Thaddeus explained.

Rufus growled. "Oh, that baby messed with the wrong dogs! Nothing scares us, not even a baby. Right, partner?"

Thaddeus sighed. "Just . . . stop."

"Thaddeus, do you think I'm bad at being bad?" Rufus asked.

Thaddeus didn't answer him. He trotted off after Bo, and Rufus followed.

Ahead of them, Dave was giving Bo directions for his shortcut. The donkey soon found himself on the top of a tall cliff overlooking a steep canyon.

"Okay, Dave, be honest. Are we lost?" Bo asked, as he slowly climbed up the narrow trail.

"No," Dave insisted.

"'Cause this doesn't exactly look like the beaten path . . . ," Bo said.

"It's a shortcut," Dave promised. "Trust me."

But Bo's next step almost sent him plummeting off the cliff! He skidded to a stop, barely keeping his balance.

"Aaaaaaaah!" Bo yelled.

"Hey! Bo! Right here!" Dave said, flapping in front of him. "Look at me, buddy. Just breathe. Breeeeathe . . ."

Bo closed his eyes, nodding frantically. He took one big, deep breath, and then opened his eyes.

"Aaaaaaaah!" he yelled again. He scrambled away from the cliff's edge and spread his legs so he was flat on the ground.

"Nope, that's it! No more of your terrible shortcuts!" Bo protested.

He started to turn around on the trail, so he could get back on the road. Then he spotted something down below, in the canyon. A caravan of travelers was heading to Bethlehem. Some were walking, others were pulling carts, and some rode on donkeys. And Mary and Joseph were with them!

"Hey, look. It's Mary!" Bo cried happily. "That's them!"

"Guess we'll have to take my terrible shortcut, then," Dave said. "You're welcome."

"Wait, no, come on, really?" Bo asked. "Which way am I supposed to go?"

"It's a cliff," Dave replied. "There's only one way to go. Down."

Dave gracefully flew down and disappeared from sight. Bo took a deep breath and began to climb down the side of the cliff. He followed the cracks and crevices in the rock, moving back and forth as he made his way down.

He couldn't get a footing on the rocks! He stumbled, tumbled, and somersaulted down, bumping into every rock he passed.

Splat! He finally landed on a nice, solid rock. He regained his footing and stood up.

A sheep was standing next to him on another rock. She grinned.

"Hi," she said. "I wouldn't stand there if I were you."

Confused, Bo looked down. The rock he had landed on was tiny, and it was stuck between two big rock formations. One false step, and he would plummet to the ground below!

"Aaaaaaah!" Bo screamed.

Chapter Twelve
It's a Sheep Thing

Frightened, Bo jumped in the air. The rock got loose and began to drop down the cliff. Bo tried to keep his balance as the rock careened faster and faster down the rocky cliffside. Thinking quickly, he bit down on a twisted tree root just as the boulder dropped out from under his feet.

He chomped down hard. The root was the only thing keeping him from plummeting into the canyon. The root started to pull out of the ground. As he tried to figure out a way to save himself, he heard a voice behind him.

"Hi, again!"

It was the sheep. She was standing on a rock ledge next to him.

"Could ynn hnnlp mnn gnt dwn! Plsss!" Bo begged.

"Just let go," she said.

Bo was confused. "Whhnat?"

"It's okay, just let go," the sheep said, but Bo was too frightened. "Here, then, let me."

The sheep bit through the root.

"Wait, nnn nnn nnn!" Bo screamed.

He fell . . . and landed safely on a ledge just a few inches below. The sheep hopped down beside him.

"I'm Ruth," she said.

"Hi, Ruth," Bo said. "I'm Bo."

He started climbing down again, stumbling and tumbling once more. Ruth walked along with him, right beside him.

"Hey, Ruth, you're a little close," Bo said. "You know? Personal space."

"Oh, sorry. Flocking," she explained. "That's a sheep thing."

She took a tiny step back from him—actually, more

of a half step. Then she stared at him, smiling.

"Ooh, this is luxurious," she said happily.

"So, what are you doing all alone on a cliff like this?" she asked.

"Well actually, I'm here with my friend Dave," Bo answered.

Ruth looked around. "Dave?" she asked. She looked at the empty space next to Bo. "Oh, hi, Bo's imaginary friend Dave. Pleasure to meet you. You sure are a fine-looking normal donkey."

"What? No, he's a dove," Bo corrected her. "And he's *real*."

"Whatever you say!" Ruth replied, although she clearly didn't believe him.

She sat down on a ledge while Bo made his way down the cliff.

"Okay, let me start over," he said. "I'm meeting Dave at the bottom. We're on the road to Bethlehem so we can catch up with my friend Mary and save her. And once we do, we'll be joining the Royal Caravan."

He hopped down to the next ledge—and found Ruth

already there, waiting for him. Her eyes were wide.

"Oh, sounds exciting!" she said. "I guess I'll get back to following the Star."

"The Star?" Bo asked. "You mean, the super bright Star?"

Bo dropped to the next ledge.

"Yeah, that one," Ruth replied. "Have you noticed that it's been getting brighter?"

"Totally," Bo agreed. "And the weird way it kind of pulsates?"

Ruth nodded. "Yes, it's like–"

"Like it means something," Bo finished for her.

The two of them made their way down the cliff as they talked. Ruth was always one step ahead of Bo.

"Exactly!" Ruth said. She leaped past him and easily jumped across a break in the rocks. "Okay, come on, we're almost down! One more chasm!" she called to Bo.

She spread her legs and planted her two left legs on one of the walls of the chasm, and her two right legs on the other wall. Once her body was wedged between each side of the gap, she expertly scrambled down the chasm. Then she settled on a rock to watch Bo.

"This is really easy for you, isn't it?" Bo asked.

"You got it, Bo! Just don't look down!" she encouraged him.

Bo tried to mimic what Ruth had done. He spread his legs as wide as he could so that his two left legs touched one side of the gap, and his two right legs touched the other side, just as Ruth had done.

"Yeah, we're going for a wedge thing here," she coached. Bo's legs were in the right position, but they wobbled like jelly. "That's it! You got it! You're a wedge! How does that feel?"

Bo answered with a terrified whimper.

"Great! Okay, just lift that hoof, and take a step down," Ruth instructed.

Bo looked down at the scary gap between his legs. "Nope," he said. "No, no, no."

"You can do it," she said calmly. "Just one hoof at a time."

Bo carefully moved one hoof away from the rock wall and lowered it to take a step down.

"That's it," Ruth coached. "Just *be* the wedge."

Bo's hoof was about to make contact, but it was so wobbly that he slipped!

"Aaaaaaah!" Bo screamed as they plummeted down the chasm.

At the bottom of the cliff, Dave was waiting for Bo, bored.

"What is taking him so long?" he wondered.

"Aaaaaaah!"

Dave looked up to see Bo falling through the chasm, flailing his legs wildly.

Whomp! He landed right on Dave!

Ruth gracefully landed on Bo's back and then bounced off him, onto the ground.

"Well, you didn't exactly stick the landing, but that was good!" Ruth complimented Bo. "You're a fast learner!"

Then Bo heard a muffled grunting sound.

"Dave?" Bo called out. "Dave!"

"I'm under you and in a lot of pain!" Dave replied.

Bo stood up and looked behind him. Poor Dave was squashed against his butt!

"Yep, I'm right here. On your butt," Dave said.

"Come on," Bo said. "Let's get moving."

Bo and Ruth trotted down the road. Dave flew to catch up.

"You must be Dave!" Ruth said happily. "I've heard great things about you. Well, *okay* things. You did leave your friend on a super dangerous cliff."

She whispered to Dave. "And he cannot climb." Then she smiled. "But hello and I am Ruth!"

"Pleasure," Dave said. "Well, we've got places to be, people to save, caravans to join. See ya."

"Thanks, Ruth," Bo added.

He smiled and walked on, leaving Ruth behind. He and Bo continued for a bit when Ruth suddenly appeared in front of them.

"Have either of you actually been to Bethlehem?" she asked.

"I've never been anywhere before," Bo admitted.

"Well, you're in for a treat," Ruth said. "The Samaritan mountains are beautiful this time of year. Deadly steep, but great views."

Bo stopped. "You've been to Bethlehem?"

"Are you kidding?" Ruth replied. "I grew up around here! I know all the shortcuts. The ins and outs. How to avoid thieves and predators, and treacherous high cliffs."

Bo looked at Dave.

"Treacherous high cliffs. You're not really considering this, are you?" Dave asked.

Bo nodded at Ruth. "Come on, Ruth. Take the lead."

Ruth gave a happy hop. "Sheep are usually better at following, but I will do my best. Let's go, flock!"

The three of them continued on the road to Bethlehem together . . . while the Hunter and his dogs silently followed on their trail.

Chapter Thirteen
King Herod's Plan

Back at King Herod's palace, the wise men's three camels had escaped from their stable. Now they were sneaking toward the palace. Deborah led the way, followed by Cyrus, and then Felix, who was dragging his feet.

"Come on, Felix!" Cyrus urged his friend.

"Shouldn't we be sneaking out?" Felix asked. "Why are we sneaking *in*?"

"Because King Herod is up to something," Deborah answered. "And we're gonna find out what. Just gotta distract that guard."

She kicked a rock into the throne room. *Clang!* The

rock hit the guard's helmet and he dropped, knocked out cold.

"Come on, hurry!" Deborah whispered.

The three camels quietly entered the throne room. King Herod was talking to his chamberlain and his scribes.

"Still no report from my hunter?" the King was asking. "Has he found the child?"

"No, sire," the chamberlain replied. "But your scribes are ready to present their findings."

King Herod grunted. "Finally, *someone's* doing their job!"

"According to the prophecy, Your Majesty, the new King is to be born in Bethlehem," one of the scribes said.

"And, that's all?" the King asked. "To what family? Who are they? *I* am the only King of Judea. If you people can't find this one child, then I'll just have to kill them all!"

Deborah turned to Cyrus and Felix. "See? I told you!" she whispered.

"Shhh," Cyrus warned.

"Shall we send soldiers to track him down?" the chamberlain asked.

"No," King Herod replied, thoughtfully considering his plan. Then he spotted the three wise men walking past the palace.

"You three! Come!" he cried.

"It's the wise men!" Deborah cried.

"Hide! Quickly!" Cyrus urged.

Caspar approached King Herod. "Any word of the new King?" the wise man asked.

"Yes. Look for him in Bethlehem," the King replied. "You are free to go."

Balthazar bowed his head. "Our humblest thanks, Your Majesty."

"When you find him, send word to me," King Herod instructed. Then he smiled strangely. "I dearly wish to know where he is, so that I may honor him . . . with a gift."

He plucked a flower from an arrangement next to his throne. He sniffed it—and then crumpled it and tossed it onto the floor.

Cyrus eyed the broken flower. "You know, I think he might be up to something," he guessed.

"I know what's happening! He's using the wise men to hunt down the new King!" Deborah realized.

"Yeah, and plus, did you see him crumple that flower?" Felix added in a loud voice.

"Be quiet!" Deborah hissed.

"We have to warn the new King," Cyrus said.

"Pack your bags, boys," Deborah told them. "Looks like we're going to Bethlehem!"

Chapter Fourteen
Saving Mary

Dave perched on Bo's back as they made their way down the road, trying to catch up with the travelers headed to Bethlehem. Ruth followed behind them, chatting the whole time.

"On the left, you'll see the field where I had my first kiss," she told them. "It was with my mother. But she wasn't an affectionate sheep, so it meant a lot to me."

Dave rolled his eyes.

"And up ahead you'll see some bushes," Ruth continued. "You may be wondering if the berries are poisonous, and the answer is . . . I don't know."

Dave glared at Bo. "I'll never forgive you for this," he said.

Bo ran ahead and looked out over the pass. He spotted Mary and Joseph in the distance.

"There they are! Come on!" he urged.

Bo and Ruth broke into a run. Up ahead, Joseph and Mary were making their way across the rough, bumpy road. Mary walked alongside Joseph, who pulled the cart behind him.

"Mary, are you sure you don't want to sit in the cart?" Joseph asked.

"No, it's hard enough for you as it is," Mary replied. "Just let me fix my boot."

Joseph set down the cart and turned to grab Mary's hand. Then his eyes got wide.

"I don't believe it," he said.

"Really, I'm fine," Mary assured him.

"No, not that," Joseph replied. "That!"

He pointed down the road. Mary turned to see Bo running toward them, with Ruth by his side, and Dave flying overhead.

"Bo?" Mary asked, in disbelief.

"Mary, you're in danger!" Bo warned. "You need to

listen to what I'm about to say *extremely* carefully!"

Bo went on to tell Mary about the Hunter and the scary dogs and how her baby was in danger. But Mary only heard the sound of a donkey braying. She stared at him.

"Do you ever feel like he's trying to talk to us?" Mary asked.

"Why is he here?" Joseph wondered.

Bo stopped. "Ugh! She's not getting it!" He turned to Dave and Ruth. "Okay, uh, new plan. Can you two act like dogs?"

"What do *you* think?" Dave asked. He was a great performer. He could impersonate anything!

"Uhh, yes! I do a great dog!" Ruth answered. "Dogs are my fourth best animal!"

Bo nodded. "Great. Just follow my lead."

Because Mary couldn't understand Bo's words, he needed to act out the danger for her. He folded his ears down so that they looked like the covering Mary wore on her head. "Look at me, I'm Mary! I'm sooo pregnant!" he said in a high voice.

Then he rubbed his head on the ground, so that the hair on his head looked fuzzy and curly.

"I'm Joseph! I'm in a bad mood!" Bo said.

"Wait, is that supposed to be me?" Joseph asked.

Mary tried not to laugh. "It's totally you!"

Bo pretended to be Mary again. "Oh no, look! Here come the dogs!"

Bo nodded to Ruth and Dave. "That's you guys!"

Ruth started to pant and wag her tail. "Uh . . . *woof, woof!* Throw me a stick and I'll bring it right back!"

Then she turned her head to look at her tail. "What's this. A tail? Ooh, I'm gonna get you, tail!"

She started to run in circles, chasing her own tail like a dog would. Dave rolled his eyes.

"Seriously, we're doing this instead of the Royal Caravan?" he asked, and then he flew away.

"No Ruth!" Bo told her. "You're a scary dog! Just be meaner!"

"Meaner? You mean like this?" Ruth asked.

She made a really scary face and snarled like a mad dog. Then she pounced on Bo.

Bo kept pretending to be Mary. "Oh no, they've got me! All is lost!"

Mary and Joseph stared at Bo.

"There's something seriously wrong with these animals," Joseph said.

Mary frowned thoughtfully. "I think Bo's trying to tell us something."

Ruth and Bo jumped up.

"Come on! Come on!" Bo urged Mary.

Mary leaned toward him. "I think he wants . . . a belly rub!"

"What? No!" Bo yelled. "I mean, yes, always, but not now. Ugh. This isn't working!"

Dave flew back and pointed down the road with his wing.

"Guys, I hate to break this up, but we've got trouble!" he shouted.

Bo and Ruth looked down the road. In the distance, they saw the Hunter and his dogs making their way through the crowds.

"Oh, those guys?" Ruth asked. "Yeah, they've been

following us since we came down the cliff!"

"Couldn't you have pointed that out sooner?" Dave asked.

"Oh no!" Bo cried. "They followed us right to her."

"Why don't we hide with that big flock over there? That's what a sheep would do," Ruth suggested. She nodded at a large group of travelers gathered around a well. Vendors were selling food.

"Great idea!" Bo agreed.

Bo bit down on the end of Mary's shawl and looped the end of it around her wrist. Then he pulled her down the road.

"Bo, what are you . . . Joseph!" she called out.

"Right behind you!" Joseph yelled.

He picked up the cart and jogged after them. Ruth and Dave followed. Bo didn't stop moving until he got to the well.

"Wow, he must be really thirsty!" Mary remarked, when Joseph caught up. She took a bucket from the cart. "I'm going to grab some water. Do you want some?"

"Sure. I guess I'll take a look at that wheel, then," Joseph said. He pulled the cart to a small hill so he could work on it, and put a stone under the wheel to keep it from rolling away.

Mary began to fill the bucket with water from the well. Bo, Ruth, and Dave got a drink of water from a nearby trough. Bo studied the crowd, looking for signs of the Hunter.

"Do you see anything?" Bo asked.

"What are we looking for?" Ruth asked.

Dave groaned. "Here we are, minutes away from being chopped into tiny little pieces by a knife-wielding psycho. We could have been riding with royalty, but no, you wanted to babysit humans!"

"I, for one, *love* babysitting," Ruth said.

Bo gasped. "Look!"

He saw a big, hulking figure pass through the crowd. Was that the Hunter?

"They're here!" he cried. "Dave, let's try to lead them away. Ruth, you stay here and guard Mary. If they find her, let us know."

Bo ran away, and Dave flew after him.

"We should have a secret signal!" Ruth called out.

"Sounds great!" Bo called behind him.

Bo charged into the crowd, searching for the Hunter. Then he spotted the tall, hulking figure with broad shoulders he had seen before.

But it wasn't the Hunter! It was a man carrying a goat on his shoulders.

Bo started to look through the crowd again.

Back at the well, Ruth spotted the Hunter's dogs.

"Oh no. He's here!" she exclaimed. "He's here! The signal!"

She inhaled, and then let out a scream.

"Aaaaaaaah!"

Bo's head spun around. The dogs were standing a few feet behind Mary, barking loudly. The Hunter looped the chain attached to their collars around a post and slowly approached Mary. Bo could see the knife gleam in his hand.

"Noooo!" he cried.

"I'll handle this," Dave said. "Looks like it's up to me!"

He flew toward the Hunter. The big man looked up at Dave and glared. Dave did a U-turn in midair.

"Nope," he said. He flew over to Ruth. "Ruth, looks like it's up to you!"

"Me?" Ruth asked. "I knew this day would come."

Then her eyes narrowed. "For the flock," she said.

She ran up to the Hunter.

"For the flooooooock!" she cried.

The Hunter brushed her aside with his foot and kept creeping toward Mary.

Bo thought quickly. He trotted over to Joseph's wagon and kicked out the rock that was keeping it in place.

Bo watched the cart roll down the hill. In a few seconds it would hit the Hunter.

But then a man pushed a wagon right into the cart's path. *Bam!* The cart crashed into the wagon.

The wagon fell over, bumping into a food stand. The stand fell over, knocking down the one next to it. Then the next stand came crashing down. People screamed, and fruit, bread, and eggs rolled across the sand.

Mary looked up to watch the commotion. The Hunter took one more step closer. He raised his arm to strike her with his knife.

Bam! Another food stand toppled over–and this one crashed down on the Hunter. He fell right into the well!

"Yes!" Bo cheered.

He ran to Mary and started braying loudly. Then he chomped down onto her dress and started to try to pull her away.

"Bo, are you okay?" Mary asked. "What has gotten into you?"

By then a crowd of people had gathered around the well, pointing at Bo.

"That donkey did it!" one man yelled. "He destroyed everything!"

Mary look at Bo. "Did you do this?"

Bo scrunched up his face, embarrassed.

Mary sighed. "Oh boy."

She led him away from the well. Ruth joined them.

"Bo! We stopped him! That went great, right?" she asked eagerly.

Dave swooped in and shouted at the dogs, who were still chained to a post.

"Hey, ya big mutts!" he taunted them.

Thaddeus strained against his chain. "Come here!"

Dave just grinned. "Hope your boss knows how to swim!"

Rufus snarled. "You just messed with the big dogs!"

He lunged at Bo, but the chain pulled him back.

"What's the matter, fellas? All tied up?" Dave teased. He landed on a fence and started to do a victory dance, shaking his tail feathers.

The dogs snapped at him.

"That's it! You're dead!" Thaddeus yelled.

"I'm so angry, but I can't look away!" Rufus wailed.

Thaddeus strained even harder, nearly reaching Dave's tail. The dove froze for a beat, then hopped one step away and shook his tail once more before flapping away.

"I hate that dancing bird," Thaddeus growled.

"I know," said Rufus. "He's so talented."

He flew toward Bo, who was racing through the

crowd without watching where he was going. Then Bo suddenly bumped into a pair of legs. He looked up.

It was Joseph, and boy, did he look angry.

"Uh-oh," Bo said.

Chapter Fifteen
Leaving the Flock

Joseph pulled the cart, which held Mary and the few supplies they hadn't lost when the cart went crashing down the hill. Bo, Dave, and Ruth trailed behind them.

"Joseph," Mary began.

"No, no, I do not want that donkey near you or the baby!" Joseph said firmly.

He looked back at Bo and shooed him away with one hand.

"Go! Get outta here!"

Bo felt sad. He had just saved Mary's life. Didn't Joseph understand how much he loved Mary?

"Joseph, it's fine," Mary said kindly.

"Fine?" Joseph asked. "Mary, this is not going well. I just promised four people I'd repair the carts that *he* smashed."

"Yeah, trying to save *her* life," Dave whispered to Bo.

Ruth felt bad for Bo. "Maybe if you pulled the cart, Joseph would want you to stay," she suggested.

"He's just too much to deal with," Joseph told Mary.

"He's just a donkey," Mary said.

"Just a donkey?" Joseph asked. "Yeah, he is just a good-for-nothing donkey who has only ever brought us trouble."

Bo stopped walking. Dave and Ruth stopped too.

"Come on, Dave," Bo said quietly. "Let's go."

He turned and started walking in the opposite direction. Dave flew onto his shoulder.

"Um, where are we going?" Dave asked.

"Where do you think?" Bo replied. "To the Royal Caravan. Where we'll finally get to do something important."

Ruth still hadn't moved. She watched Mary and Joseph go off one way, and Bo and Dave go off the other way.

Then she hurried to catch up with Bo. "Hey, Bo. Wait a minute," she said. "What about the Star? It means something; you said so yourself."

"You follow the Star," Bo replied. "I'm done with that."

"But . . . what about our tiny flock?" Ruth asked. "Flocks stick together."

"We're not a flock," Bo said. "I never should have followed you."

Ruth stopped, stunned and hurt. Dave stared at Bo. He'd never heard his friend be mean before.

Bo kept walking, and Dave flew to join him. The two friends left Ruth behind.

That's when Mary realized Bo was gone.

"Bo? Bo!" she called out.

Bo heard her, but he didn't turn around. He walked and walked across the desert, not saying a word. He walked up and down the sandy hills. He walked until he couldn't walk anymore, and then he collapsed with exhaustion.

Then his ears twitched. He heard the sound of bells jingling. He looked up.

"Is that the Royal Caravan?" he asked.

Dave flew up to get a better look. "I can see them!"

Bo hurried up the next hill so he could see too. Dave landed on his shoulder. There, crossing the next hill, was a long parade of tall horses, people in brightly colored clothing, and fancy wagons. The Royal Caravan!

Excited, Bo charged down the hill. The bandage came loose from his leg and got picked up by the wind. Bo watched it fly away–toward the brightly burning Star.

He stopped. He was so close to the caravan. So close. But what had he left behind?

"The Royal Caravan! The Royal Caravan!" Dave cheered.

"Dave, I don't think I can go with you," Bo said quietly.

Dave smiled. "Of course you can! What do you mean?"

"Look, I know we've always talked about joining the Royal Caravan," Bo began. "Seeing the world. Being part of something important. But now that we're here . . . I don't think this is it. Mary may not be big and royal, but she's important. To me. I know this was your dream, and even though I can't go, I think you should go. Without me. I'll be fine."

He paused. "Say hi to the horses for me."

Dave glared at Bo, angry. He shook his head. Finally, he spat out a reply.

"Aw, come on!"

"No really," Bo said. "I mean it."

"Bo, yes, you're right," Dave said. "The Royal Caravan was our dream. But the best part was . . . that it was gonna be *us*."

Bo stared at his friend. Did he really mean that much to Dave?

"If all I wanted was to flap around a bunch of fancy wagons, I could have gone and done that a while ago. I mean, I can fly, you know. You realize that."

Bo nodded. "Yeah, I guess so."

"I had more fun watching you walk in circles than I'd ever have with those stuck-up nags," Dave said. "So look, you lead the way, and wherever you go, your best friend, Dave, will be right behind you."

They both paused to gaze at the caravan as it made its way toward Rome. Bo took a deep breath. He and Dave both turned to look up at the Star, which shone more brightly in the sky than ever before.

"You ready?" Bo asked.

While Bo and Dave were walking across the desert, a crowd had gathered around the well. The rope dangling into the well creaked and shuddered.

Then the Hunter's massive hands appeared, grasping the edge of the well. He still held his gleaming knife in one hand. He pulled himself up and ran to the dogs.

"We're gonna die! We're gonna die!" Rufus wailed.

Whack! The Hunter slashed through the post with his knife, freeing the chain.

"We're gonna live! We're gonna live!" Rufus cheered.

Thaddeus narrowed his eyes. "*Someone's* gonna die."

Chapter Sixteen
Breaking Down

Joseph pulled the cart toward Bethlehem. Mary looked behind, hoping that Bo would show up. But she only saw his friend the sheep.

Suddenly, one of the wheels on the cart struck a rock. Joseph yanked the wheel over the rock, but when it slammed back down, he heard a loud snap. The wheel's axle broke in half, and the cart tipped over. Some of their belongings spilled out onto the road.

"No, no, no!" Joseph cried, frustrated.

"Let me help," Mary offered.

She climbed out of the wagon.

"Mary, you're in no condition to help," Joseph said as

he crouched down to examine the broken axle.

"Stop saying that," Mary said. "I'm fine!"

Joseph stood up. "No, you are not fine! None of this is fine!"

"Joseph, God chose us," Mary reminded him.

"But why? Why us?" Joseph asked. "Look at us! We'll be lucky just to make it to Bethlehem. And we're supposed to raise the Son of God?"

Mary listened. She understood Joseph's point.

"This must be part of God's plan," she said.

Joseph frowned. "Well, so far this plan is going great! I can't wait to see what happens next!"

He knelt down again and turned his attention to the cart. Mary walked away. The sun was setting and a mist had risen up from the sand.

Ruth nervously approached Joseph and smiled.

"What are you looking at?" he asked crossly.

Ruth scurried away and hid behind the broken cart. She watched as Joseph tried to fix it, and another piece snapped. Joseph dropped to his knees, and then looked up at the heavens, closing his eyes in prayer.

"Lord, I can't do this," he said. "I am not the father of a king. I am just a carpenter. Please give me a sign."

At that moment, he felt something on his shoulder, and opened his eyes to see Bo nudging him, with Dave perched on his back. Joseph looked back up at the heavens.

"Really? The donkey?"

Bo pushed Joseph harder. Joseph stood up and picked up one of the bundles. Bo pushed him again, in the direction that Mary went.

Joseph finally got it. He looked into the mist.

"Mary?" he asked.

He dropped the bundle and hurried down the road to find his wife. Ruth poked her head out from behind the cart.

"Hi, Ruth," Bo said.

Still hurt, Ruth just stared at Bo.

"Look, I'm sorry for what I said back there," Bo said. "It was mean. And I'm glad we followed you."

"Really?" Ruth asked. "Oh, that's so good to hear, because once I saw the Star I tried to get my flock to follow me, but they wouldn't. So I struck out on my own, which has been hard 'cause, well, I'm a sheep." She smiled at them. "Thank you for coming back."

"Yeah, well, don't read too much into it," Dave replied, but it was clear he was happy to see Ruth again too.

Bo smiled. He nodded toward Mary and Joseph's things. "Can you help me with these? For Mary?"

"Of course!" Ruth replied. "Good leaders are always willing to lend a hand."

Dave frowned. "I am done with this one," he muttered under his breath.

As the animals got to work, Joseph hurried to find Mary. He found her sitting at the foot of a hill.

He ran to her side. "Mary, are you okay? I'm so sorry."

She turned to him with tears in her eyes. "No, Joseph. You were right."

"I was?" Joseph asked. "About what?"

"This *is* hard," Mary replied. "Trust me, I know it is. Just because God has a plan, doesn't mean it's going to be easy. And that scares me."

"Hey, I'm scared too," Joseph admitted. "But I'm

here. And I'm yours. And I will give everything I have to keep you and the baby safe."

He took her hand and kissed it. She smiled.

"I mean, it may not be a lot, but . . ."

A wind picked up, clearing the mist. On the other side of the hill, they could see the road to Bethlehem.

"Uh, speaking of which, what happened to all our stuff?" Mary asked.

Joseph looked behind them, remembering that he had left the broken cart. But just then, Bo, Dave, and Ruth appeared. Bo was carrying all their bundles on his back!

Mary gasped. "Bo!" she cried happily.

"I always did like that donkey," Joseph said. "I always did. I didn't say it enough, that's true."

"Oof!" Mary suddenly exclaimed. "Hello!"

"Did the baby kick?" Joseph asked.

"No, that was something different," Mary said, looking into his eyes.

"Different? What different?" Joseph asked. "Like, *baby's coming now* different?"

Mary nodded. "We've got some time. But, yeah. I think so."

Joseph stood up and started moving in circles.

"Okay, nobody panic!" he cried. He started pulling bundles off Bo's back. "I've got the clothes, I've got the bag, I've got the sheep–why do I have the sheep?"

In his excitement, he had accidentally picked up Ruth. He put her back down.

He cleared off the rest of the bundles.

"Bo, can you carry her?" he asked.

Bo nodded. Joseph helped Mary climb onto the donkey's back. He hoisted the bundles over his shoulder.

Then Mary, Joseph, Bo, Dave, and Ruth continued down the road, following the Star.

Chapter Seventeen
No Room at the Inn

Along with Mary, Joseph, and Bo, people from all over headed to Bethlehem to be counted for the census. Among the weary travelers were the three wise men, moving through the desert on their camels. The Hunter was headed there too, holding Rufus and Thaddeus on a chain.

When Mary and Joseph arrived, it was nighttime, and the small town was overcrowded. Long lines of people waited in front of the census table.

Bo pulled up in front of a nearby inn. Joseph helped Mary off the cart and brought her inside. Bo looked around, searching for any signs of trouble. He looked up to the sky to get comfort from the Star, but it was covered by storm clouds.

"Aaaaand, they're in the inn!" Dave cheered. "Thank goodness. This has been so stressful. Hoo! Don't know how I held it together."

"Well, we made it," Ruth said happily. "Safe and sound in Bethlehem."

Bo frowned. "Something's not right."

He looked up and briefly saw the Star as the clouds parted. When he looked back down—he saw the Miller staring at him! Bo gasped.

"You!" the Miller shouted.

"No, no, no!" Bo wailed.

"Easy, easy, it's okay," the Miller said. "Just hold still!"

Before Bo could get away, the Miller lunged at him. He slipped a rope around Bo's neck.

"Let me go!" Bo yelled.

Dave flew into the Miller's face.

"Oh no, you don't, you crazy-eyed donkey-eating miller. That's my best friend!" he cried.

The Miller swatted Dave away, and he fell to the

ground. Ruth ran over and helped him up with her snout.

"Dave, are you okay?" she asked. Then she raised her head. "Where'd they go? Who *was* that?"

"Bad news," Dave answered.

Meanwhile, inside the inn, Mary and Joseph were speaking to the innkeeper.

"I'm sorry, the inn is full," he told them.

"What? No, can't you see? She's about to have a child," Joseph pleaded.

The innkeeper shrugged. "What can I do? Blame the census."

He motioned to the hallway, where a number of guests were asleep on mats.

Joseph looked at Mary, concerned. Then he had an idea.

"You know what? We'll pay double! Just hold that thought! I'll be right back!" he said. "I left the money with Bo."

He ran out of the inn and then stopped, shocked.

"Bo? Where's Bo?"

The donkey was gone, along with all their bags! His face turned pale with fear. Dave flapped his wings, trying to get Joseph's attention. Ruth *baaaa*'ed at him.

Mary staggered out of the inn, taking short, quick breaths.

"Joseph, we're running out of time!" she warned.

"Mary!" Joseph cried. He rushed to her side to help her.

Ruth ran down the street and Dave flew above her. They were both in a panic.

"Bo! Where are you?" Ruth yelled.

"Ruth, I know we have had our personal issues, but we need to set them aside and find Bo," Dave said.

"We have personal issues?" Ruth asked, puzzled. "Dave, I think you are a delight!"

Dave grinned. "I am a delight. Thank you for noticing." Then he pointed forward. "Okay, time to activate Operation Rescue Bo!"

Up ahead, the Miller dragged Bo toward a stable. At the same time, Bo could see the Hunter and his dogs enter the town.

"You're going back to the mill, donkey!" the Miller said.

"What? No, no, no!" Bo protested.

The Miller dragged him away, and he watched, helpless as the Hunter and his dogs made their way toward Mary. They stopped in front of the inn. Thaddeus sniffed the door.

"She's here," he said.

But Mary and Joseph had already left that inn. The couple had tried another inn, but that was full too.

"Where do we go now?" Mary wondered.

"We'll just have to keep looking," Joseph said.

As they walked off down the road, the three wise men entered the town. They led their camels by the reins.

"So this is Bethleham!" Felix said.

"It's pronounced Bethle*hem*," Cyrus corrected him.

"That's what I said. Bethleham," Felix repeated.

"HEM," Cyrus corrected him again. "As in 'ahem,' as though clearing the throat."

"That's what I've been saying!" Felix protested. He shook his head. "You need to get your ears checked."

"Boys, focus!" Deborah scolded. "We gotta find the new King and tell him he's in danger."

"Right, let's go find him!" Felix said.

The three camels tried to walk off–but they realized that the wise men had tied their reins to a fountain.

"Ack! They've secured our restraints!" Cyrus complained.

"Yeah, and they tied us up too!" Felix added.

"We have to find the new King!" Deborah said anxiously.

They watched the wise men walk into Bethlehem and start knocking on doors.

Cyrus shook his head. "Wise men, indeed!"

"We'll never find him if we're tied up here," Deborah said. "We have to go out and search!"

"That's it!" Felix said. "I'm biting through the reins."

Cyrus gasped. "You wouldn't dare. That's fine Corinthian leather. It's expensive."

"You kidding me?" Felix asked. He looked to Deborah for moral support.

"No, Cyrus is right," Deborah said.

"We'll have to untie the knots ourselves," Cyrus said. "First, Felix, we'll need you in the middle. Deborah on the far left."

The camels awkwardly stepped over one another, ducking under one another's reins.

"No, the other left," Cyrus said.

"You mean right?" Deborah asked.

Soon, they were tied together in a giant tangled knot.

Nearby, the Miller pulled Bo into a stable. He roughly tied Bo to a post in the middle of a barn.

"No, no! Don't do this, please!" Bo begged. He pulled against the rope, but it wouldn't break.

The Miller left, and Bo kept pulling and pulling. "I can't let down Mary and Joseph," he said.

Defeated, he stopped pulling. He dropped his head in complete despair.

Then he began to pray.

"God, hello, um, I don't really know how this works," he said. "Or if you listen to prayers from donkeys, but I've seen Mary do this many times and I don't know what else to do. I need to help them. I'll walk in circles for the rest of my life in that mill if you want me to! Just please let me go help my friends!"

Bo sighed. Then suddenly, from out of the darkness, a voice spoke.

"Who is that?"

Chapter Eighteen
New Friends

"God?" Bo asked.

A goat with bulging eyes stepped out of the shadows. He had a patchy gray, brown, and white coat.

"I'm freaking out here!" the goat wailed. "I'm seeing things, guys! There's a donkey in the corner and he's talking to God and he won't stop looking at me!"

A cow with a smooth brown coat stepped up next to the goat.

"Zach! Pull yourself together!" she told the goat. Then she nodded to Bo. "What's your name, sweetie?"

"Bo," the donkey replied.

A gray-haired horse emerged from the back of the stable.

"Bo is a funny word," she said in a dreamy voice. "Bo. Bo, bo. Boooo. Bo, bo, bo . . ."

Bo eyed the three barn animals.

"Oh, I'm doomed," he groaned.

"I'm Edith," the cow said, "and Zach and Leah aren't usually like this. You caught us at a bad time."

Leah giggled. "Yeah, we haven't slept in nine months."

Bo's eyes widened. "Nine months?"

"Not a wink!" Zach confirmed.

Bo nodded. "Oh, so that explains your eyes."

"What? What's wrong with my eyes?" Zach asked, his eyes spinning wildly in his head.

Bo didn't want to upset him. "Nothing."

"Yep, no sleep at all since that giant night-light turned on," Edith explained.

"Light?" Bo asked.

"Every single night," Zach explained. "It's making us a little crazy."

Edith nodded her head, motioning for Bo to follow her. The four animals walked around a wall in the stable.

"Ta-daaa!" Edith said.

Incredibly bright light from the Star shone into the stable, directly on a wooden food trough filled with hay–a manger. The light shining on it illuminated the manger with a miraculous glow.

"*Aaaaaaaah!*" Leah sang. "Sorry, so excited. Zach and Edith don't like the spotlight, but I think it's beautiful."

The sight filled Bo with excitement. "It's here!" he said. "I can't believe this!"

"Me neither," Edith said with a sigh.

"You don't understand," Bo told her. "That light–that's the Star! This is where it's been leading me. But . . . Mary, Joseph."

Bo knew he had to get Mary and Joseph to the stable somehow. He turned to the animals.

"Guys, I gotta get out of here. Can you help me?" Bo asked, looking down at the rope around his neck.

"I'll chew him free!" Zach cheered.

Zach walked up to Bo–but instead of chewing on the rope, he started chomping on the wooden post the rope was tied to.

"Woody," Zach complained.

"Wait, no," Bo said. "Try biting–"

Leah interrupted him. "I know! I'll sing you free!"

She started singing random, joyful notes.

"That was beautiful, but not helpful," Bo said, feeling more anxious by the minute.

Zach stuck out his tongue. "I dink I got a thplinter in my tongue."

"Step aside," Edith said. Then she bit down on the rope, freeing Bo from the post.

"Yes! That's perfect!" Bo cheered. "Now I just gotta get past that gate."

He lowered his head and charged the gate, ramming it. The gate didn't budge, and he fell back, dizzy.

"Has that ever worked for you?" Edith asked.

"No, actually," Bo admitted.

The three animals lined up against the stable gate. First Zach, then Edith, then Leah. Bo climbed up on each one like he was climbing up steps. Then he hopped over the gate.

"Thanks, guys!" Bo said. "I'll be back. Get the place ready. Mary's having a baby!"

"I love babies!" Leah squealed.

Edith sighed. "Great. Now we'll never sleep."

Bo charged down the street, searching for Mary. He turned a corner—and ran right into Dave and Ruth!

"Oh, hey, Bo," Ruth said calmly. Then it hit her—they'd found their lost friend. She gasped. "Bo!"

"Ruth!" Bo cried.

"Bo, you're here!" Dave said happily. "We've gotta help Mary and Joseph."

"I know," Bo said. "Where are they?"

"We don't know," Ruth admitted.

"The dogs are here," Bo informed them. "We can't take them on our own. We have to find help!"

"You can count on us, Bo!" Dave said.

"We won't let you down!" Ruth promised.

Bo turned and ran down the road. Dave and Ruth took off in two different directions.

Dave frantically flapped his wings, darting around people and animals.

"We're not going to stop those giant scary dogs with a fluffy sheep and a tiny donkey," he muttered. "Even with a very masculine and brave dove."

He scanned the travelers and frowned. "We need backup. Where do you find a dog-eating hippopotamus in Bethlehem?"

He wasn't paying attention to where he was flying, and he crashed right into a camel. He fell to the ground—and looked up to see the three camels, still tangled together in their reins.

"A three-headed camel? Nice!" Dave cried happily. "Guys, you gotta help me. My best friend's up against two vicious dogs and this bloodthirsty maniac with a long knife and a helmet who's seriously straight out of your nightmares."

Felix looked at Deborah. "Are you hearing this little guy?" He had to be talking about the Hunter and his dogs—the one who was after the new King!

While Dave convinced the camels to help them, Ruth ran to the green hills outside of town.

"Help! Help! Anybody!" she yelled.

Then she stopped. Just over the hill she spotted a flock of sheep grazing in the grass while a shepherd watched over them.

"Oh, look, a flock of sheep," she said, and then she realized something. "Oh, that's my f-f-f-flock!"

She looked around. "Help? Is there anybody else? No? Okay."

She took a deep breath. "Bo needs my help," she said. It didn't matter that she and her flock hadn't agreed on things in the past. Bo needed help, and these sheep could help him.

"Bo needs my help. Bo needs my help. Bo needs my help," she repeated as she ran to the meadow.

"H-h-h-h-heeeeey, everybody," Ruth said. "What's up? It's me, Ruth! Do you remember me?"

A few sheep looked up. Then every member of the flock took two steps back, away from Ruth.

Ruth took a deep breath. This was going to be harder than she thought.

"Okay," Ruth said. "Guys, I know you thought I was crazy when I went following that Star, but you wouldn't believe all the adventures I've had out there."

The sheep just stared at her.

"And the biggest one of all is happening tonight!" Ruth continued. "I've made new friends, and they need our help."

The sheep ignored her. Ruth climbed up onto a rock.

"So this time you gotta follow me," she told them.

A few sheep stared blankly at her. Ruth started to feel angry.

"Guys, this is IMPORTANT!" she yelled.

She stomped her hoof on the rock. A jagged streak of lightning shot down from the clouds and hit the ground behind her.

The sheep looked up at Ruth, surprised. She looked down at her hoof. Had she done that?

A wind kicked up. Blue particles of light descended from the heavens and lit up the meadow. Behind Ruth, a chorus of winged angels appeared. Ruth looked behind her and stared at them in awe.

One of the angels looked directly at the shepherd.

"Fear not. I bring tidings of great joy," the angel said.

"For unto you is born this day a Savior, Christ the Lord."

The flock of sheep looked from the shepherd to the angels. Then they all stared at Ruth.

"Told you it was important!" Ruth said.

Chapter Nineteen
Away in a Manger

Mary and Joseph still didn't know the King's hunter and his dogs were after them. They walked through the streets of Bethlehem, knocking on doors. They had to find a safe place for Mary to have the baby.

After another door slammed in their faces, Mary put a hand to her belly.

"Joseph, I can't go any farther," she said.

"Okay," Joseph said. "Uh, here."

He took off his cloak and laid it on the ground. Then he helped Mary lie down on it and lean back against the house.

"Mary, look at me!" he said. His voice was commanding,

but calm. "You're doing great. Remember: God chose us for a reason. This must be part of His plan."

Mary nodded. Joseph turned away from her and began to pray in a low voice.

"Help us. Help us. Please, God, help us."

Storm clouds swept across the sky, covering the Star. Bo ran through Bethlehem, looking for Mary and Joseph.

Suddenly, he heard distant barking. He hurried to the edge of a cliff overlooking the town square and skidded to a stop.

He looked right and he saw the Hunter and his dogs!

"Not good," Bo said.

Then he looked left and saw Mary and Joseph, alone on a street corner. The Hunter would reach them in just minutes.

"Oh no. That's not good at all," he said. "Mary! Joseph!"

He sped down the cliff and raced through the streets, jumping over baskets and bins and dodging travelers. As he neared Mary and Joseph, he began to bray urgently.

Thaddeus and Rufus heard Bo and snapped their heads in his direction. They began to bark viciously, and the Hunter drew his sword. He marched toward Mary and Joseph.

Bo tugged on Joseph's shirt.

"Bo, you're back!" Joseph greeted him. "Buddy, we need somewhere to go."

Bo had an idea. He turned away from Joseph, showing his back.

"You know a place?" Joseph asked.

Bo crouched, ready to go.

"Mary, let's go," Joseph said.

He helped Mary onto the donkey's back. As soon as she was settled, Bo broke into a run. Joseph ran beside him.

Bo ran faster than he'd ever run before, heading back to the stable. He looked up and saw the clouds part, revealing the Star. He ran even faster.

They quickly arrived at the stable. Joseph opened the gate and then helped Mary off Bo's back. Bo rushed inside.

"Guys! Guys! Sorry to barge in, but Mary's about to have a baby!" he announced.

"They're here!" Zach said.

"I love babies!" Leah cried.

"We're all set," Edith said.

Mary and Joseph walked in.

"No, no, no," Joseph said. "This isn't going to work. We can't have the baby here, Mary. We need stronger bedding. We need warmer–"

Mary reached out and firmly grasped Joseph by the arm.

"Joseph. I'm ready," she said with a strong and confident smile.

Joseph nodded. He gently helped Mary lie down on a bed of hay. She smiled gratefully at Bo for finding the stable for them.

Bo smiled back. He looked at the stable animals.

"Thank you," he said.

Then he headed outside.

Mary still wasn't safe. There was one more thing to take care of.

Chapter Twenty
Chaaaaarge!

Bo stood in front of the stable gate, waiting. He didn't have to wait long. Rufus and Thaddeus came trotting toward him, dragging their chain behind them.

"Well, well. Look who it is," Thaddeus said.

Rufus growled. "We should have eaten him the first time we met him."

"But, Rufus, if we had eaten him, he never would have led us here," Thaddeus pointed out. He nodded at Bo. "We've been meaning to thank you. Now be a good little donkey and run along. You've served your purpose."

Bo backed away from them.

"You guys are pretty scary, and you might be stronger than I am," he began. Then he stopped firmly. "But if you want to get to my friends, you're gonna have to get past me first."

"Oo-hoo-hoo! I was hoping he was going to say that!" Rufus said, licking his lips.

The big bulldog ran toward Bo. The donkey quickly turned around and gasped.

"What is that?" Bo asked.

Confused, Rufus stopped and looked past Bo. "What's what?" he asked. Then he realized he'd been tricked. "I wasn't supposed to look was I?"

"Donkey kick!" Bo cried.

Bam! With a mighty kick, he sent Rufus flying into the air. The big dog slammed into the ground. The blow knocked him out cold.

Thaddeus snarled at Bo. "You're mine!"

He charged at Bo. Bo knew he couldn't fool this dog too. He closed his eyes, bracing himself for the worst.

Then he heard a *clang!* He opened his eyes. Thaddeus and Rufus were still connected by a chain, and the chain was stuck under Rufus's body. Thaddeus stopped just inches from Bo's face.

He snarled and snapped at Bo, who moved back toward the stable.

"Huh. I didn't even plan that," Bo said. "That was close!"

Then Thaddeus stopped snarling and sniffed. An evil grin spread across his face and he turned to look behind him. Bo followed his gaze.

The Hunter stomped up the path to the stable. Bo ran to close the gate.

As the Hunter walked, he stepped on the handle of a cart. The end splintered off. He picked it up with one hand. With the other, he pulled a cloth from a nearby clothesline. He coiled the cloth around the wooden stick. Then he swung the stick at an oil lamp.

The lamp shattered. The Hunter's makeshift torch burned brightly.

Bo shuddered with fear. Then he gathered his courage. He galloped toward the Hunter.

"Not gonna let you do this!" Bo cried.

He lowered his head and rammed into the Hunter.

They collided, but Bo bounced right off the big man's muscular torso. The Hunter kept walking.

Bo winced. "Okay, you're big."

He galloped toward the Hunter again, but the man swung his arm and batted Bo away easily. The donkey hit the ground. As he got to his feet, he saw the Hunter moving toward the stable.

"No, no, no!" he yelled.

He ran at the Hunter again, but Thaddeus tackled him from the side. They slid toward Rufus. He pinned down Bo with one of his big feet.

"Now can I eat him?" Rufus asked.

"Very soon," Thaddeus promised.

Bo couldn't move. He watched helplessly as the Hunter opened the stable gate.

"No! Mary! Joseph!" Bo yelled.

The Hunter raised his sword. Before he stepped inside, he turned to smile at Bo.

"Mary, I'm sorry," Bo said softly.

"Baaaaaaaaaa!"

The strange sound startled the Hunter. He turned

toward it—to see Ruth jumping over a fence post!

"Chaaaaarge!" Ruth yelled.

Ruth's flock of sheep collided with the Hunter. They swept him off his feet and carried him on their backs away from the stable. They swept up the two dogs along with him.

The sheep dumped the Hunter onto a street cart. He sat up, dazed, as the wave of sheep passed. But before he could get to his feet . . .

"Dave to the rescue!"

Dave swooped down from the sky. Just below him, on the ground, the three camels came barreling toward the Hunter. They crashed into him, knocking him back into the dog chain. They pushed the Hunter and the two dogs down the alley, to the edge of a cliff.

Bo raced after them. When he arrived at the cliff, the Hunter was dangling off the edge. He tried to claw his way back up, but he kept sliding back.

Bo peered over the cliff's edge. The two dogs hung from the Hunter's leg. Their chain was wrapped around his ankle. Panicked, they tried scrambling up the wall, but the chain attached to their collars choked them, holding them back.

"Help! Somebody help!" Thaddeus yelled.

"I don't want to die!" Rufus wailed.

Bo knew that the Hunter couldn't hold on much longer. All three would die if they fell off the cliff.

Not far away, he saw scaffolding–platforms for workers building houses–going down the cliff. There might be a way to save them.

Am I really gonna do this? he asked himself.

His answer came quickly. *Yes.* If there was a way to save these lives–even though they were mean, scary lives–he would have to try.

"It's just another cliff," he told himself.

He scrambled onto a platform just below the dogs. With his mouth, he removed one of the handrails. He wedged it between the platform and the cliff.

"Grab ahold of this!" he called to the dogs.

Thaddeus and Rufus paused, unsure if they could trust him.

"Come on! You don't have much time!" Bo urged.

Thaddeus looked up at the Hunter, who was about to lose his grip at any moment. Thaddeus turned back to Rufus and nodded.

Rufus swung for the rail and managed to grab it with his two front legs.

"I got it!" Bo cried.

Suddenly, they heard the sound of a newborn baby crying. The Hunter tried once again to pull himself over the top of the cliff. That's when he realized that the dogs were holding him back.

The Hunter lifted his leg–and kicked off the chain wrapped around his ankle.

The two dogs fell. Bo dove down the cliff after them.

The Hunter planted his sword in the ground and used it to pull himself up. He was about to get to his feet when the crack in the earth that he'd created with his sword widened. The chunk of the cliff under his feet broke off. He tumbled down the rocky slope and disappeared into the darkness below.

Dave, Ruth, and the camels rushed to the edge to look down.

"Bo?" Dave called out.

He flew down, and discovered Bo wedged between two pieces of rock in the cliff. He had the dog chain in his mouth, and Thaddeus and Rufus dangled beneath him.

Slowly, Bo made his way up the jagged cliffside. He took one step. Then another.

"Bo, you're doing it!" Dave cheered. "Ruth, a little help!"

"All right, listen up, sheep!" Ruth called to her flock. "Start climbing!"

She looked down at Bo. "Excellent climbing form, Bo! Keep it tight!"

One of the sheep passed her. "Taught him everything I know," Ruth bragged.

The flock of sheep scrambled down the cliff and helped Bo pull the two dogs up to the top of the cliff. The three camels took the chain from Bo as he neared the top and pulled the dogs to safety.

The animals surrounded the dogs, eyeing them suspiciously. The dogs panted and wheezed, exhausted.

Bo wearily turned to the camels and then nodded toward the dogs. Cyrus, Deborah, and Felix leaned down and bit the dog collars off the necks of the dogs. The chains fell away. The dogs looked shamefully at Bo.

"We're bad dogs," Rufus said.

"You don't have to be," Bo told him. "You're free now."

Thaddeus and Rufus looked at each other, amazed. Bo nodded to them and then turned and started to run.

"Bo! Where are you going?" Ruth called out.

"We've got a baby to meet! Come on!" he urged.

The camels looked at one another.

"After all that, it *is* a baby shower," Cyrus said. "I was right this whole time!"

"I was right too!" Felix protested. "It's a birthday party! It's the day of his birth!"

Deborah shook her head. "I'm gonna let them have this one," she said.

Then the three camels followed Bo, Dave, Ruth, and the sheep to the stable.

Chapter Twenty-One
A Child Is Born

A peaceful hush fell over the stable, interrupted only by the sound of a baby crying.

Bo slowly approached. The light from the Star illuminated one corner of the stable. Bo walked past Zach, Leah, and Edith to Mary, who was lying back in the hay, cradling a baby in her arms. Joseph knelt next to them.

"Hey, little guy," Bo said.

Mary handed the baby to Joseph. He held the baby out toward Bo. The donkey leaned in curiously, and the baby's tiny arms brushed his snout. Bo jumped back, startled.

Joseph laughed, with tears of joy glistening in his eyes.

"It's okay, Bo," he said. He stood up and gently laid the baby in the manger full of hay.

All the animals had gathered in the manger to watch. Even little Abby, the pygmy jerboa, had found her way there. She climbed onto Deborah's head.

"You know, I was there when this whole thing got started," she bragged in Deborah's ear.

"Everyone, this is Mary and Joseph," Bo announced. "And that's their new baby."

"The flock is growing," Dave said with a smile at Ruth.

Thaddeus and Rufus slowly padded in. The other animals tensed up, suspicious, and blocked their path. Bo studied them. Their eyes looked sad and sorry—not scary.

"It's okay," Bo said. "Let them in."

The two dogs walked up to the manger and looked at the sleeping infant.

"See? He's just a baby," Bo said.

The two dogs felt their hearts melt as they gazed at the baby.

"Aw, look at him!" Rufus said sweetly.

They turned to leave, nodding at Bo.

"So, are we good dogs now?" Thaddeus asked Rufus.

The bulldog smiled at him. "We have to try."

The three wise men walked in next, holding their gifts. They smiled at Mary and Joseph. It didn't matter that this baby, the Messiah, had been born in a stable. The Star had led them here, and that was all that mattered.

"I'm sorry, is this your stable?" Joseph asked.

"No," Balthazar replied. "We've come to honor the new King."

"I'm sorry, *king*?" Bo asked, confused. "Why does everyone keep talking about a king? What king?"

The three wise men knelt before the baby in the manger.

"What's his name?" Caspar asked.

Mary smiled proudly. "His name is Jesus."

The wise men presented their gifts.

"For Jesus. Gold," Balthazar said.

"Myrrh," Caspar said.

Melchior presented a small pottery jar. "Do you guys like frankincense?" he asked. "I never know what to get."

"Thank you," Joseph said.

"For the newborn King," Balthazar said, and all three bowed toward Baby Jesus.

Bo couldn't believe it. All this time, Mary had been carrying a king in her belly! He gazed back at the animals in the stable. All of them were bowing before the child.

Bo bowed his head.

"Guys!" he whispered to Dave and Ruth. "I carried a king on my back!"

"We're never gonna hear the end of this are we?" Dave whispered back.

Ruth smiled. "And I hope we never do."

"Yeah, okay. Me too," Dave admitted.

The whole sight moved Deborah the camel.

"You know, I think people are going to remember this night. This moment," she said. "What happened here around this manger will be celebrated for thousands of years. Families will come together and exchange presents, have feasts, and sing carols. All to remember the grace of this moment that we are witnessing right now."

Her words hung in the air for a moment–and then Cyrus and Felix began to chuckle.

"Okay, Deborah," Cyrus said, shaking his head.

"She's back to talking crazy again," Felix said.

Baby Jesus started crying again, and Mary stood and picked him up.

"Thank you," she told the wise men.

She sat back down on the bed of hay, and Joseph joined her. Mary motioned for Bo to join them. He suddenly realized how tired he was. He limped over and plopped down next to her.

She stroked his head. "What have you been up to all night, Bo?" she asked.

Bo looked at Mary. *Long story,* he thought. *And one*

I'll never be able to tell you. But that's okay. Because we're all safe. You, me, Joseph, and Baby Jesus, the newborn King.

Outside, the bright Star faded away.